safekeeping

safekeeping

Karen Hesse

FEIWEL AND FRIENDS

NEW YORK

A FEIWEL AND FRIENDS BOOK
An Imprint of Macmillan

SAFEKEEPING. Copyright © 2012 by Karen Hesse. All rights reserved. Printed
in the United States of America by R. R. Donnelley & Sons Company,
Harrisonburg, Virginia. For information, address Feiwel and Friends,
175 Fifth Avenue, New York, N.Y. 10010.

Library of Congress Cataloging-in-Publication Data Available

ISBN: 978-1-250-01134-3

Book design by Ashley Halsey

Photo on page 287 by Mariam Diallo

Feiwel and Friends logo designed by Filomena Tuosto

First Edition: 2012

10   9   8   7   6   5   4   3   2   1

macteenbooks.com

This book is dedicated to
the children of Haiti

part one

I stare out the small window over a vast field of clouds.

New travel restrictions ban even backpacks from the cabin of the plane.

I haven't brought much out of Haiti anyway. The orphans at Paradis des Enfants need my sandals, my toothpaste, my T-shirts more than I need them.

Besides, Mom will buy new stuff for me when I get home.

I can't believe half of what I've heard in Haiti about what's happening in the U.S. But if even *half* of that is true . . .

My heart raps at my ribs like a trapped thing.

I remember my parents warning that all hell would break loose once the American People's Party took power.

And now it seems as if all hell *has* broken loose.

The plane is rerouted in flight with no explanation. To Philadelphia. When we touch down in Philly military personnel direct us through customs. There are three separate officers at three discrete stations. Each station has its own arsenal of weaponry. Each its own computerized lists.

At the second checkpoint, soldiers single out a dread-locked man three people ahead of me in line and strong-arm him away. He had been sitting across the aisle from me on the flight from Haiti. I watch, stunned, as the man is led off, arrested on suspicion of . . . of what?

My head aches by the time my turn comes at the last station. The officer carefully studies my passport, shines a small light on it, fixes a hard stare on my face. He checks my name against his master list, then opens my passport again. "Radley Parker-Hughes," he says. There's something about my name he doesn't like. I'm having trouble breathing. The room spins around me.

Finally, he makes a decision. He lets go of whatever it is that's bothering him and sends me through.

It's taken hours to clear customs. Racing across the terminal, I fear I'll miss my reassigned flight. But at the designated gate I discover the plane to Manchester, New Hamphsire has been delayed indefinitely. The attendant at the desk promises to make an announcement the moment she gets more information.

I close my eyes. As best I can I block out the news reports playing on the overhead monitors. I can only watch the same chaotic scenes so many times without going out of my mind.

With no cash in my pocket and my charge card in my checked backpack, I try to sleep. What other way is there to eat up the endless hours of waiting?

Except for a plastic cup of complimentary orange juice on the flight from Haiti, I haven't eaten since early this morning when Monsieur Bellamy put a piece of his wife's cake into my hands. "As soon as I get a line through, I will send a message to your parents, letting them know you are on your way," Monsieur Bellamy reassured me.

Now, nearly ten hours later, I'm still nowhere near home and they've just announced that our plane will be delayed at least another few hours.

Although my stomach has definitely grown smaller on one meal a day at the orphanage, there's a gnawing emptiness inside me.

I surrender to the overwhelming need to hear the sound of my mother's voice. But no matter how much I search I can't find a phone booth anywhere. Finally, I ask an attendant at the USAir desk.

"All the pay phones have been removed," she tells me. "No one needed them anymore. Everyone has a cell."

But with the new travel restrictions no one is allowed to carry cell phones onto the plane. Mine nests inside my backpack, which is in some cargo hold between Port au Prince, Haiti, and Manchester, New Hampshire.

I guess I'll just have to wait. I trust that Monsieur Bellamy has reached my parents by now and told them when and where to meet me. I hope they know my plane is delayed so they're not sitting all these hours at the airport.

Everywhere I look there are uniformed patrols. Their steely scrutiny unnerves me.

An eerie quiet fills the terminal. The only sound is the nearly muted commentary on FOX news. Everyone stares at the screens, watching the same clips of vigilante groups wandering like packs of dogs, frenzied looters racing through electronics stores, round-shouldered police interviewing shocked bystanders.

My fellow travelers sit or stand, staring, mesmerized by the images. No one speaks.

Near dawn, after an endless wait, a plane is finally found for us and we're allowed to board. A little over an hour later, we land in New Hampshire. I'm one of the first from our flight to reach baggage claim and my pack emerges from the black hole early for a change.

I'm exhausted from twenty-four hours of travel. I just want to climb into the backseat of my parents' car, eat a granola bar, close my eyes, and sleep through the two-and-a-half-hour ride home.

Despite the huge plate-glass windows in the terminal, a gray and sullen light greets me. I expected to return to the breathtaking beauty of May. Instead, out the glass doors a heavy blanket of storm clouds suffocates the life out of New England.

And I don't see my parents.

I've never arrived in an airport without my parents meeting me. They always come, day or night, no matter where I land, no matter when I land . . . they're always there.

But they're not here now.

Monsieur Bellamy promised to get a call through to them.

I reason that they'll be here any minute . . . that something has held them up. Or that they've gone to grab something to eat because they've been waiting for so long. Soon I'll see their beaming faces. Soon I'll be pawing through the hamper of snacks my mother always packs for the ride home.

But when they don't show after a half hour, I swipe at my tears, battling the rising tide of panic.

I've been unwilling to take my eyes off the doors, certain my parents will materialize at any moment; but I can't wait any longer. Stopping at a bank of chairs, I dig around for the cell phone inside my backpack.

Posted on the airport walls are new laws printed in boldface letters. Curfews. Mandatory registrations. Threats of incarceration. I don't remember seeing any of this in Philadelphia. Is it possible they've been posted only in the last few hours? Is it possible they've been posted only in New England?

When I open my cell, I remember it's dead. I reach into my backpack again, this time for the charger. But I can't remember packing the charger. Not until I've emptied every compartment twice and checked every zippered pocket a half dozen times am I certain that I left the charger in Haiti. Beside my bed. At the Paradis des Enfants.

Typical. So typical.

My parents never scold me about the frequency with which I lose things. They always just fix it for me, no matter how I screw up. I'm used to them just fixing it for me.

Where are my parents now? I need my parents to fix things for me now. But they are nowhere. They're nowhere. Even if I borrow someone's cell phone, I can't reach them if they're already on the road. They both refuse to have cells of their own. Maybe, after this, they'll agree to get one.

My hand closes on the one good surprise I've found in my backpack during my search for the charger. Jethro, one of the orphans at Paradis des Enfants, has tucked the little bear my mother knitted for him into my bag. I am too old for stuffed toys, but I am deeply grateful for this selfless gift. Jethro loved his little bear. What a sacrifice it was for him to part with it, to send it home with me. Now I know why he told everyone with such confidence that I would return. Carefully, I zipper the little bear back into my pack, take a deep breath, and walk out into the damp, chill air.

Striking up a conversation at curbside with a couple that left Haiti the same time I did, I learn they live an hour north of Manchester. He's a carpenter and she's a nurse and they've just spent six weeks volunteering in Port au Prince as part of a pledge they made to their church.

Usually I'm not bold, but these people, clearly struggling to handle their excess of luggage, seem safe enough. And I'm still trying to kill time, still waiting for my parents to show up. I offer to go back in and search for one of those metal luggage carts for them. They thank me and watch as I disappear back inside the terminal.

But there are no carts to be found.

Staring out at them through the glass doors, I make a decision. It's looking more and more like my parents aren't going to show. It's possible Monsieur Bellamy couldn't get through, that they don't know I'm here.

When I return to the couple I propose helping them with their bags.

I ask, in exchange, if they could give me a lift to the bus station in town.

I've got my charge card now. I can buy a ticket home. It'll be a great surprise for my parents when I walk through the front door.

Just the suggestion of my getting into their car causes fear to flicker across the face of the wife. All these new rules have set everyone on edge. But the grateful husband says, "Sure, we can give you a ride."

We locate their car on the long-term lot. I'm crammed into the backseat with their luggage shifting around me. On the floor, as I squeeze in, I catch the glint of coins.

Bending over, pretending to retie the heavy boots my parents bought for me to take to Haiti, the boots I never wore the entire time I was there, I pick up two quarters from the car floor and slip them into my sock.

It's only fifty cents. The man would have given it to me. But my cheeks feel hot as I sit back up. I can't believe what I've just done.

The man keeps talking. They haven't noticed that I've stolen their quarters.

He's heard the Internet has been shut down. "The government trying to stop demonstrations on the street," he suggests.

They are careful not to be too critical.

"The government is trying its best," the wife says. "Under the circumstances . . ."

———

There are concrete barriers all around the bus station. The man pulls up as close to the door as he can.

"Take care," he calls as I leave the car, hoisting my pack up onto my shoulder. I feel the quarters rub against my ankle.

"You, too," I call back. "Thanks for everything."

———

The Manchester Transportation Center swarms with soldiers and U.S. Marshals, just like the airport. I spot a pay phone, finally, inside the station and call home using the stolen quarters.

A recording comes on informing me that I've reached a nonworking number. I try to remember other phone numbers, numbers for my aunt in Atlanta, my cousins in Florida, my friend, Janine.

But I never memorized any of those numbers. They were programmed into my cell.

And my cell is dead.

It's been a month since I've heard my parents' voices; about two weeks since their last postcard.

On the front of that card was an image of our cat, Romulus, hanging over the arm of our sofa. On the back my mother had written, "I've got claws and I know how to use them."

It was those words, and then no word at all, and then the assassination of the president of the United States that sent me running home.

I vow to myself that tomorrow Dad and I will go out and get a new charger and this time I'll never lose it. I also vow to memorize important phone numbers from now on. Or at least write them down somewhere and carry them with me.

In the bus station, announcements repeat over a loudspeaker.

"All passengers must submit to a security check before boarding. Travelers wishing to board must first present a completed travel request form. Please have a valid I.D. ready to show. There will be no crossing of state lines without prior government approval. We repeat. There will be no crossing of state lines without prior government approval."

I turn to the man standing beside me. He's wearing a shabby suit and scuffed leather shoes; his long, dark hair is threaded with gray.

"Travel request forms?" I ask. "No crossing state lines?"

"Yeah," he says. "You don't have your papers?"

"I've got a passport, I've got a credit card."

"Where've you been? Under a rock? You're not getting anywhere without authorized travel papers."

I step out of my place in line and attach myself to a group of students leaving the station.

This is madness.

This is the United States.

This doesn't happen here.

But it is happening.

I can't get hold of my parents by phone and without the proper paperwork I can't take the bus.

I've got to get home. Government approval could take days, weeks.

I can't wait that long. Once I'm home everything will be all right. My parents will know what to do.

I just have to get home.

I find a phone booth at a nearby mini-mart and try calling home again. Same message.

You have reached a nonworking number.

I ask inside the store for a map of New Hampshire.

The guy at the register is tapping away at the counter with a pair of chopsticks. He looks my age, seventeen. Maybe a year older. "Those maps down there are free," he says, pointing with a chopstick to a row of brightly colored maps in a wire rack.

Free is good. I open the complimentary map. It's loaded with advertisements.

"I'm heading west," I say. "Maybe on back roads . . ."

"In this part of the state there's really only one road running east to west." He squints at the map for a moment or two, then traces a route with his chopstick. "Route 101. It's a fairly straight shot."

"How's the best way to get there?"

He shrugs, embarrassed. "I don't actually know. I don't live in Manchester, just work here. I live in the next town over. Hey, Joanie?"

A middle-aged woman wearing a maroon mini-mart smock comes from somewhere between the aisles. She wears her dyed red hair in a ponytail, her gray roots showing. Her eyes are the color of robin's eggs.

"101?" she asks. She draws a map on a napkin she's plucked from the hot dog counter. "It's not hard, but it's a hike getting there from here."

She has no idea how far I need to go.

"That's okay," I say. "I like walking. Thanks." Besides, I

think, Monsieur Bellamy could get through to my parents any time. They could be driving like mad at this very moment, trying to find me.

"Anything else?" the guy asks.

It's been more than a day since I've had any food in my stomach. I put a huge handful of granola bars on the counter and pull out my charge card.

"Sorry," the guy says. "Cash only right now. The lines to the credit card companies are down."

I put the granola bars back on the shelf.

He slides a pack of gum under my hand.

"I can't pay . . ." I'm afraid to surrender the quarters. They're all I have.

"It's on me," he says, waving me out the door.

I worry about the boy and the surveillance camera and whether he'll get into trouble for giving me a pack of gum.

His supervisor, Joanie, has vanished into the aisles. But I wonder if she's witnessed what just happened.

My mother wouldn't have let me accept the gum. In fact, when I get home, she'll probably insist on driving back here to pay for it.

At Paradis des Enfants they would break one stick of chewing gum into a dozen pieces so everyone could have a taste.

It's not until I've been walking for an hour or so that I realize the boy at the mini-mart could have called the police on me for shoplifting as I went out the door. It could have been a setup. It wasn't. But it could have been.

I was lucky this time, I guess. Still, I can't rely on luck.

I have to be smarter from now on. I have to think from every angle.

———

I make myself walk purposefully, not too fast, not too slow. But then my mind wanders and my pace quickens. I keep thinking about last Friday when Monsieur Bellamy rushed to the orphanage.

"Radley," he cried, breathless. "Radley, someone has assassinated your president!"

Usually I laughed at the ridiculous rumors that masqueraded as "news" from the U.S. But this wasn't funny.

Monsieur Bellamy paced, agitated. "There have been arrests. Many arrests."

I thought about my mother's last card and her comment about having claws and knowing how to use them.

Running to my tiny room on the second floor of the orphanage, I retrieved my cell phone to call my parents, to make certain they were all right. But my cell phone was dead then, too, and there was no power at the orphanage to recharge it.

Monsieur Bellamy said it didn't matter. Phone lines to the U.S. were down anyway.

All I could think of was my parents, what was happening to my parents?

———

I realize I am walking too fast, calling attention to myself. "Slow down. Slow down, Radley," I whisper.

I'm surprised by the small amount of traffic for a city as big as Manchester.

I've passed several storefronts but most look dark.

Coming through a residential area, I hear a dog bark occasionally. But there is a general, unnerving quiet.

I see very few people. When I do pass someone, we avoid making eye contact.

———

In Bedford, I follow a small trail into a clump of trees and spit out the piece of gum I've been chomping since leaving the mini-mart hours ago. A searing pain hammers in my right temple. I sit and rest and study the map. I'm hoping to see some way of reaching home sooner. But the guy at the mini-mart was right; there really is only one road to take and I should stay on it anyway, in case my parents come.

I imagine myself walking the thin red line of Route 101 from Bedford to Keene, then Keene to Brattleboro, and finally walking down Putney Road to my front door.

It's too far.

Stop it, I tell myself.

But it's too far.

Maybe you'll get a ride. Mom and Dad could show up at any moment. But even if Monsieur Bellamy doesn't get through to them, maybe someone will recognize you from home. Quit making it out to be the end of the world. You'll get there. Everything will be okay.

Footsteps sound somewhere behind me and I realize how vulnerable I am, isolating myself on this narrow path. I'm afraid to turn and look at the person approaching.

Kneeling, I get a good hold on my backpack, trying to act nonchalant. I think I can spin around and stun someone with it if I have to.

While I pretend to be getting something out of my pack, the footsteps come right up on me. Then a man and his dog blow past. They don't even acknowledge me.

I rise, brush the grass and dirt off my pants, return to the road.

In my head, I am spinning a lie about who I am and what I'm doing. It would be easier to tell the truth. Dad would advise me to tell the truth. But I remember that last officer in customs and how he reacted to my name and I'm afraid to tell the truth.

———

I can smell food before I see the restaurant entrance. I'm mad crazy hungry now. How long has it been since I've had anything in my mouth but gum? If only I had a little emergency money left. My parents sent me with plenty of cash. But I spent it all. I've never been good at holding on to money. All I have is the fifty cents I stole from the couple at the airport.

I hadn't thought about how I'd eat when I gave Monsieur Bellamy the money for the plane ticket. Or where I'd sleep. I just assumed my parents . . .

Until I went to Haiti, I'd never gone for more than a few waking hours without food. Then, at the orphanage, I learned to get by on one meal a day . . . just like the children . . . just like Therese, the laundress, and Eulalie, the nurse.

It was hard at first.

At home I lost my temper when I got too hungry. My mother always carried snacks in her purse so I wouldn't turn mean. In Haiti, I just barely managed to be civil at first on an empty stomach. But in time my body got used to it.

I don't know how long a person can go without eating. One of the orphans, Delphine, a small girl with dark, thoughtful eyes, was pulled from the rubble on the sixth day after the earthquake. Six days buried under the wreckage of a building with no food or water. If she could survive that, I can do this.

At least I can cup my hands under the faucets of gas station sinks and drink. Delphine couldn't do that.

I stand outside the restaurant. There are only a few cars in the parking lot. My stomach is red-hot with hunger.

The day is starting to fade and I notice there are no lights going on.

Entering the dim restaurant, I ask if they've got any food they were going to throw away. The waitress glares at me, disgusted. She yells at me to get out.

My heart is pounding and I can't see straight as I stumble back into the parking lot. People have always been so kind to me. Given me things, even before I asked for them.

I'm halfway across the lot when a girl about my age catches up with me. "Look," she says. "Linda isn't usually like that. I don't know. Everything's so crazy right now. It's just there've been so many people begging. There's a

Weathervane a few miles down the road," she says. "My brother works there. He'll help you . . . give you something to eat. They've got a generator running full-time there. They'll be open right up to curfew. My brother says they're throwing tons of food away. Just don't get caught out after curfew, okay." Then, embarrassed, she hands me a soiled napkin with something wrapped inside and veers away.

I hold the napkin carefully. If it's still a few miles to the Weathervane, I can't walk fast enough to beat curfew. Whatever is inside the napkin will have to do for tonight.

Unwrapping the bundle with shaking hands, I find the crusts from three slices of pizza. It's more than I could have hoped for. I silently thank the girl.

While gratefully gnawing my way through the first two crusts, I manage another mile or so. As dusk cloaks the road in shadow, I slip into the woods behind the Hill Brook Hotel.

All day the sky has threatened but not until I'm in under the trees does a light rain begin to fall.

As I sit on the edge of the woods, chewing the last crust of pizza, listening to the tap of rain on new leaves, it dawns on me how long this night will be. I know I shouldn't take it out and expose it to the weather, but I ignore common sense and slip my hand into the zippered compartment where Jethro stashed his little bear.

I didn't know how soft it was. I wonder if all the knitted dolls my mother makes for the orphans are this soft. I hold the bear against my cheek, press it against my closed lids, take comfort from it, before tucking it safely away in my backpack again.

By now the rain has penetrated through the leaf cover, soaking me to the skin. It's not even midnight, I think, and I'm dripping wet. And I'm cold.

And I'm scared.

And I've never been so alone, not in all my life.

I think about the children at Paradis des Enfants, how they wanted to come and sleep in my bed with me and I didn't let them. How their little bodies, all elbows and ribs, pressed against me as I sat on the edge of their cots and wished them good night.

I long for them now. For the smell of them, for the feel of them leaning into me.

I'm so exhausted; my legs burn from walking, my stomach burns from hunger. But my brain won't shut down.

———

The night is endless. I think and think. About my mom and dad, about my room at home, about Chloe and Janine, about Romulus, about teachers at school, and the children at Paradis des Enfants.

I play over and over my conversation last Friday with Monsieur Bellamy. He swore to me that it was impossible to get a ticket back to the U.S.

"But my parents . . ."

"They are adults. They can care for themselves. You are safer here right now."

"But I'm needed there."

"You are needed *here*, Radley. Everyone abandons these children. Do not turn your back on them."

"You can't keep me here, Monsieur Bellamy. I'm a volunteer. If I want to go home I should be allowed to go."

It took all the money I had, leaving only a few coins for Eulalie to buy bread for the children when they complained of their stomachs aching.

I told Monsieur Bellamy that I hadn't been able to reach my parents to tell them I was coming. I told him at least three times.

He looked so sad. "It is very difficult in America now. If it is *too* dangerous, you must go to Canada. Do you hear me, Radley?"

Was that yesterday morning? Could that possibly be only a day and a half ago?

Haiti seems like a dream now as I shiver inside the woods somewhere between Manchester, New Hampshire, and home.

I remember how the children followed me to the gate of the orphanage. It was hard to leave them.

When the gate swung shut behind me, separating us, I heard them weeping in the yard. I heard the sound of them over the concrete wall.

And then Jethro began to sing.

I sit in these woods in New Hampshire remembering the sound of Jethro's voice following me down the road. I slip my finger into the half-zippered compartment of my backpack and touch the small, damp bear, and I am filled with an indescribable sorrow.

———

I steal out of the woods at dawn. After walking yesterday in neighborhoods, the road today feels so desolate and empty. The rain has stopped but I'm wet from sitting all night in it and I'm stiff and sore from yesterday's march. And I'm tired. My eyelids feel like they're lined with sandpaper. And now black flies have started swarming around my head.

After less than an hour I come on a small food market. Inside, I use the restroom to wash up. The power seems to have come back on again.

I think about asking for food but I can't bring myself to do it, not after the waitress yesterday. I'll have to get to the Weathervane. It can't be much farther.

But once I do get there I don't know what to do. It's too early in the morning for anyone to be there yet. There are no cars in the parking lot. The restaurant isn't opened and won't be for hours.

I retrace my steps back to the road and start walking again.

Except for the occasional cluster of retail stores, I'm surrounded by forest. The road is an endless conduit for camo-colored military vehicles, long lines of them.

I force myself to act like a kid walking to school. There are a couple of us out here on foot with packs on our backs so I'm not as unique as I feared.

I order my aching, exhausted body to go on.

A few pizza crusts and a pack of gum. I had more to eat in Haiti.

Each vehicle that approaches, either from the east or

west, I check for the green plates of Vermont, hoping someone I know is behind the wheel.

When I stop to rest throughout the day, my legs tremble stupidly. I think, at least my shoes fit, remembering how careful Mom was. Making certain the boots didn't rub. Insisting I wear them around the house for a few days before packing them to go to Haiti.

By the time I stop for the second day, I'm hollow as a bone and my head throbs. I want food. I want a shower. I want a flush toilet. I smell bad and I feel worse. More than anything I want my parents. I have tried every pay phone along the road but there aren't many and even fewer that work. The last time I tried, I got a new message. *This number is temporarily out of service.* I'm hoping whatever is messing with the phone lines will be repaired by tomorrow and I can call home. My parents could be here in less than two hours, assuming they've got the papers they need to cross state lines.

I prepare for another night in the dense, damp, cold woods, wedging myself against a tree. Pulling my knees up, I rest my chin on my bony kneecaps and scratch my bug bites. I unzip the bear and press him against my stomach. Keeping pressure there helps to ease the hunger. I think about my bed in Haiti. I think about rice and beans and bathing babies in sun-warmed rainwater. I have to be smarter about this. Tomorrow I have to spend the night under some sort of shelter if my parents don't find me. Tomorrow I have to eat.

Eventually I nod off.

Sometime during the night I wake, fully alert. I hear

footsteps running along the gravel shoulder. It sounds like someone moving fast. There is the quiet hum of a motor, as if someone is driving slowly behind the runner. Then the motor cuts out, doors slam, and I hear multiple sets of feet pounding the ground.

Almost as quickly as a scream begins, it's silenced. There is only the sound of fists against flesh.

After the car peels away, I think I should get up, leave my hiding place, check on the person by the side of the road. But somehow I can't make myself leave the safety of the woods. And I cannot stop trembling.

———

I am so cautious when I emerge from the trees at dawn, but there is no one lying on the shoulder and no one waiting for a new victim. Whatever happened during the night belongs to the night.

I feel grateful the fists didn't find me, and then hate myself for feeling that way.

This is my third day on the road and in that time I have had water to drink and gum to chew, three crusts of pizza, and nothing more.

I don't know how far I've gone; it's just one step after another. I've stopped swatting at the flies. It takes too much energy. I let them swarm. I let them bite. And I keep going until I see a woman sitting in a car on the shoulder of the road.

She's eating a sandwich, staring out her front windshield.

My feet won't go on. I can't take my eyes off her sandwich.

She sees me.

I am having trouble standing. The ground moves beneath me.

The woman leans out of her car window.

"What are you staring at?" She wipes a smear of mustard from the side of her mouth with the tip of her index finger. I watch how her hand moves, how her sandwich moves. I watch everything that has to do with that sandwich. "Quit staring at me," the woman yells.

"Hungry," I say. "I'm . . . hungry."

She squints, holding the last bites of sandwich in her hand. She motions me over to the car. She is not kind, I can see that in her eyes, I can hear it in her voice.

I am afraid to come close to her but I am too hungry not to come. I venture only so far and reach out my hand but there is still a space between us. My hand is shaking.

"Here," she says, thrusting what's left of her sandwich out the window, tossing it toward me.

My reactions are slow. The sandwich, what's left of it, lands in the road. I stare at it.

"I thought you were close enough," she says. There is nothing nasty in her voice now.

Trembling, I bend down and pick up what's left of the sandwich, bread crusts, a sliver of meat, a drop of mustard.

Road dirt and all, I shove it into my mouth, stumbling back across the road away from her.

After a couple of miles, I veer off 101, cutting a small corner from my journey and come through the town of Milford.

I smell food again.

Not long after a restaurant comes into view. But I am afraid to go in. Something makes me hold on to my fifty cents. Something keeps me from walking through the door and begging.

I slip around the back of the restaurant instead. In the middle of the day, cautiously, I edge up to the Dumpster. As silently as I am able, I lift the lid and grope inside, pulling out the first plastic bag that comes to hand.

I thought this would be harder. I look around to see if anyone is watching, rip the plastic open, shove food into my mouth. While I'm chewing I fill my pockets with food. The Dumpster stinks. It makes my stomach rise.

I throw the ripped bag back into the Dumpster, lower the lid, look around again, and though my heart is racing, I walk coolly away from this thing I have done.

Ten minutes down the road I duck into a small grove of trees and throw up everything I've eaten.

No sooner does the heaving stop, I reach into my right pocket and, a little more slowly this time, begin to eat. French fries, cold, stained red with ketchup. Few things have ever tasted this good. I eat three. Then two more. I'm eating more slowly now, walking more evenly.

I watch eagerly for the next Dumpster.

———

By the time I reach the village of Marlborough I start recognizing certain landmarks.

There's a used bookstore here. They carry every subject you could possibly imagine, including photography books, even some of my mother's. She's crazy about the place. We drive over here once a year, sometimes more. It takes less than an hour by car to get here from home.

I walk past the bookstore now, glancing toward the shelves of paperbacks on the porch.

The shelves are still there, the books are still there. But the shop looks abandoned.

A radio plays in the mini-mart where I use the bathroom. Instead of music, they have a news station tuned in. Stories include a shooting at a Claremont grocery store, a sniper picking off National Guardsmen in Concord, a body found in the Ashuelot River.

The girl at the mini-mart eyes me suspiciously as I hover in an aisle, listening.

A rack of newspapers stand at the door. One of the headlines reads: MAN CAPTURED CROSSING STATE LINES.

I hold out my fifty cents and will my hand not to tremble. "You got any food I could buy for this?"

She points to a display of plastic-wrapped sweets, two for a dollar. I study them. Then shake my head no and leave the store.

I've already raided her Dumpster, stowing my take in my backpack. She can keep her plastic candy. I can keep my fifty cents.

———

When the commercial stretch of Keene comes into view I know I'm close.

I'm tired, I reek. Though I wash up in gas stations and mini-marts and fast-food places, I still look pretty road worn.

I have a ridiculous sense of pride at having made it this far. My parents will love this story once they get over the shock.

I keep walking despite the approach of night, hiding when I hear a car coming. It's just so hard to stop now.

I long to be settled in my own home, sitting across the table from my parents, talking about everything that's happened over the last few weeks in their world, in mine.

But I'd never make it the whole way in the dark along this stretch without being arrested for breaking curfew or attacked by thugs.

I hate stopping when I'm this close but it's insane to go on.

Taking shelter away from the yards of barking dogs, away from curious eyes, away from the knots of vigilantes trolling this section of Route 9, I wait out the night.

———

In the early hours of the morning I begin the final leg of my journey.

By afternoon, there is one long hill remaining between me and Vermont, between me and Brattleboro. One long hill cut eons ago by the Connecticut River. But I can't cross state lines without the proper papers. Instead, I step off the road into a wooded stretch of land and wait for dark. Jethro's bear waits with me through the hobbled hours.

Around two in the morning I zip the bear back into his pocket, and cautiously, my heart drumming in the hollow of my throat, I approach the bridge over the Connecticut River.

There is a guard booth on the New Hampshire side. But it's empty.

I crawl over the pedestrian bridge, the old bridge over the Connecticut, expecting a bullet biting into my flesh at any moment. But I am halfway across, then all the way across. And no one, nothing has stopped me.

As I emerge from under the railroad bridge on the Vermont side of the river and edge through the darkness, onto Putney Road, joy overtakes the fear. I am almost home.

I should wait until dawn, until curfew ends. I should find a hiding place and sit out the rest of the night. But I can't.

Not one vehicle passes me. I don't know whether it's because of the gas shortage or the curfew, but I'm grateful to know that something in this crazy new world is working for me.

I am less than five minutes from the house, from my parents, when I hear the growl of a car. Headlights are just coming around the corner. Another moment and they'll see me.

I dive behind a fence on Putney Road. A dog begins barking. But the dog is quickly hushed. And the headlights sweep past.

Just when I am about to congratulate myself, I realize someone is watching from their upstairs window. I can see only the outline of a person, but I'm certain I'm being watched. I hold still, very still, and finally the curtain twitches and the person is gone.

Afraid to linger a moment longer, I slip out from behind the fence and quickly make my way to the Common.

Minutes later, I move silently up Channing Street, catching sight, at last, of home.

After all of these days of walking, I'm giddy with relief to see the silhouettes of those familiar chimneys in the gray dawn.

I step over a dark stain in the street as the eastern sky lightens.

At last I will be with my mother and father, protected by them. I'll be clean again. Have regular food again. Soon everything will be back to normal.

The sight of the house thrills me. My father's gardens appear as they always do this time of year, breathtakingly beautiful, with the crab apple blossoms fragrant in the dawn air. I stand in awe for a moment. The azaleas bloom beside the porch steps in wondrous profusion.

In the driveway, my mother's car, my father's truck, just as they should be.

"They're here," I whisper as I climb onto the porch. "They're home."

———

I don't have my key so I lean on the bell. Dad would never be up this time of day but Mom will be.

When no one answers, I try the doorknob. It turns

easily . . . this enormous door that always sticks in humid weather . . . it opens with the slightest push as if it's been expecting me.

By the light from the approaching dawn I see my reflection in the big front hall mirror.

I take a moment for a general damage report, surprised that I don't look worse considering how I feel. I want to look okay when they first see me. I want my parents to be proud, not horrified.

"Mom?" I call. "Dad?"

The house answers with an unnerving silence.

Sensing movement outside. I peer through the sheer curtains. Two policemen in uniform get out of their vehicle at the end of our front walk.

It's dawn. Why are they here? It's as if they've been waiting for me.

I throw the lock on the door and rush up the stairs, hoping, with each step, that I will catch sight of my mother, my father, that one of them will beckon me silently to safety.

But not even Romulus shows his face.

As I reach the attic, the part of the house exclusively Mom's, I hear pounding at the front door. Looking for a place to vanish, I search all the angles, all the nooks of my mother's workspace. None offer the concealment I need. And then I remember the crawl space under the eaves.

Because there is no knob or latch to pull it open, I use my fingernails to pry the door from the wall, fold myself in half and creep inside the airless space. I pull the door back into the wall and hunker down.

My father finished this little room years ago when he

remodeled the attic for Mom. He said it gave him access to wires in the ceiling of the floor below.

Crouching, I wait, my nostrils filled with my own stench. I concentrate on my breathing, willing my chest to fill and empty. But I can do nothing to still the wave of panic flooding me as the police continue to pound on the front door two floors below. I wonder if the hammering of my heart is truly as loud as it is in my own ears.

Finally, the police give up. I wait in the airless space under the eaves. When I feel safe enough to emerge, I crawl across the wood floor and seek comfort under my mother's desk. Cowering there, I wait for my parents to come out of hiding.

———

There's not a sound in the house. Not the entire day. I'm afraid the police have left someone behind to watch so I wait until night has filled every corner of the attic. When the house is completely dark, when the street is utterly still, I begin a methodical search of every room, on every floor.

No sign of my parents anywhere. My mother's camera and wallet are gone from the front hall. But my father's CPAP, the thing he uses to help him breathe at night, is still at his bedside. There's no sign of Romulus.

I look for a note, for a clue, as I search each room. I find nothing.

In the kitchen I open the refrigerator door, forgetting about the light coming on. But no light comes on. Instead, the foul odor of spoiled food smacks me squarely in the face. My stomach is empty but the stench still makes me gag.

Slamming the refrigerator door shut, I flee from the kitchen where the smell of rot now overwhelms the room. Climbing up to the second floor, I grab the flashlight from Dad's nightstand and gather clothes from my closet, collecting bits of my life to carry back to the nest I am making for myself in the attic.

In my mother's office everything remains as I remember it. The mess my mother apologizes to visitors about but never cleans up. The desk clock Dad made for Mom out of wood from our old butternut tree. The tiny music box I brought her from Paris. I stroke the satin pouch with my mother's knitting needles, I run my fingers over her old cameras. I pounce on my mother's address book. Phone numbers, at last. But when I pick up the phone on my mother's desk, it's dead.

Surrounded by familiar objects, I try to sleep, but I'm hungry.

Padding all the way back down to the kitchen I find the stench has mostly abated. Dad's assorted bags of chips and pretzels fill a basket on the granite countertop. Grabbing the basket, I head back up to the attic.

Ever since I left Haiti I held only this one plan . . . to get home, to be with my parents. Finally I am where my parents should be. But they're not here.

I keep turning over options, like a fisherman looking for worms under stones, but I find only empty holes.

———

I wake clutching Jethro's bear, jolted from sleep by the sound of banging at the front door, two floors below. Angling myself to peer from the attic window, I grip the sill and gaze out.

The police have returned. I'm not sure why they're looking for me. I don't know why they start their day so obscenely early.

But I don't intend to find out.

Even after they give up and go away, I am afraid to go outside in daylight.

Instead, I spend hours in the house, spying out the window, watching for a familiar face below, someone, anyone who might help. But there are few people passing, and none I recognize.

If only I could safely run out and knock on doors, find a sympathetic friend, someone who could tell me where my parents are. But it's not safe to go out. Not with the police looking for me. Only after dark do I dare prowl the eerie streets. In this town, because of my parents, because of my mother's celebrity, I am known by enough people to be recognized and turned over to the police.

All day I have thought about how few friends I have. If this had happened two years ago, I would have gone straight to Chloe. But Chloe is gone.

The only other person I'm close to is Janine. Under cover of night, like a missile, I lock in on her place, a few blocks from my house, making my way through a darkness unfamiliar in Brattleboro. Not a streetlight, not a house light shining.

I tell myself Janine will know what to do. She's older,

wiser. Maybe she'll even know where my parents are. It will be so good to see her. And maybe her toilet flushes.

I can see dimly as I make my way through the inhospitable dark. Occasionally I'm aware of others moving around me in the night but some sixth sense allows us to avoid each other.

Feeling my way blindly up the stairs to Janine's apartment, I tap lightly at her door. No answer.

I'm afraid to knock harder, afraid of drawing the attention of the other tenants in the building. I try tapping again, then reach for the knob and twist, but the door is locked. It doesn't budge.

I tap once more and wait. I'm met only with a dense silence. Maybe, when this all began, Janine moved back to her parents' house. I wouldn't blame her. But I can't go to find her there. Her father had American People's Party signs all over his front lawn. He held a fund-raiser for the APPs in his living room. I wouldn't be safe there.

Climbing back down the steps, I use my hands to find my way. Finally, I stumble down the last flight, and when I'm confident I'm not being watched, I slip out of Janine's building.

Afraid to push my luck any further, sliding along through the shadows, swallowing down my disappointment, I make my way back to my empty house.

———

My life settles into a surreal routine. At random times each day the police park outside the house, stride up the front path, climb the porch steps, and pound on the door. Each day I press against the attic wall, hidden from sight, my heart thudding, waiting for them to go away. They have not forced the door yet. I wonder how long until they do.

After they've gone I spend some time watching out the window, some time going through my things, my parents' things.

I consume everything in the pantry, everything that can be eaten without cooking: canned tuna, canned peaches and pears, an entire jar of peanut butter. I even eat Romulus's cat food.

––––

Our street used to be so busy. People took Channing to bypass Main Street, admiring the small, well-kept gardens.

The gardens of Channing Street are no longer well-kept. Tall grass overshadows tangles of weeds. Faded blossoms lie on the ground, the life choked out of them.

Hardly anyone makes their way up Channing Street now. And those who do look straight ahead, minding their own business.

––––

After waiting and watching through another long day, in the deep night I slip out of the house. It's hunger that brings me out this time.

I've spent all day thinking about the location of Dumpsters in the neighborhood. The nearest one is behind the American Legion, only a block away. It's on a side street, and there is only one house within sight of it. I should be able to get what I need and return home quickly.

But the Legion Dumpster is empty. I move to Plan B.

The next nearest Dumpster is just a few hundred yards from here, but that puts it within sight of the police station. Best to avoid that one, I think.

Instead, I decide to cautiously make my way over to the bin beside the Putney Road Market.

I am more exposed here, right on the main drag. The market sits across from the county courthouse. But there isn't anyone going in or out of there at night, not like there is at the police station.

Still it feels as if I'm walking into the lion's den. I approach the Dumpster slowly. There is no movement, no sound, no lights, no emergency generators growling.

I gather food quickly from the bin and check to make certain no one has seen me, no one has heard me, no one is near me as I sneak back toward the safety of the house.

With my backpack full, I avoid the path in front of the courthouse where there might be cameras. Instead I return home via the Common, the site, in better times, of concerts and rallies, weddings and fairs. Now the Common looks deserted, haunted.

The tall bronze statue stands silently in the three a.m. chill. It had been placed there at the conclusion of the Civil War, erected by a grateful town that swore it would never forget the horror of neighbor pitted against neighbor.

Now the statue, green with age, rages as only bronze can, in cold frustration.

I will myself safely home, unable to shake the feeling of being watched. This time of night is for the lawless, the curfew breakers. I have been lucky so far. But I remember that night in the woods between Manchester and Brattleboro, listening to fists against flesh, witnessing with my ears a suffering that could just as easily have been my own.

I'm at the far corner of the Common, almost home, when I'm jumped. I sense my attacker only a moment before he slams hard against me and begins pulling at my pack.

Surprise unleashes my fury. I spin and grab at my attacker's hand as it scores my face. I bite down hard on thin fingers. Then kick, aiming first for the groin, then for the shins. I hear a snap, a cry of agony. I do not look back. The moment I feel my attacker let go, I pull away and tear home.

My hands tremble as I try to fit the key into the lock.

It takes several attempts.

Every few seconds I look back over my shoulder; no one is there. No one has followed me.

Back inside the house, I lock the door and bang up to the attic where I curl under my mother's desk and wait for my heart to stop pounding.

Throughout my childhood I played at being a superhero. My mother would photograph me, image after image, a mildly bemused expression on her face. What would her face reveal now, I wonder, to know the true savagery of her daughter?

Later, much later, I unpack my evening's take. Slowly I chew on sandwich crusts, on expired chips, on bruised and rotting apples.

The police have returned four times in as many hours. They are determined to take me. I'm determined to frustrate them.

There is no point remaining here. Not without my parents. Not like this.

I need a place of safety. If I stay in this house much longer I'll be taken for sure, transported to jail for no reason, like the dreadlocked man from the plane.

Monsieur Bellamy urged me to head north to Canada if things got too dangerous in the U.S. It seemed ridiculous at the time, but now waiting out this madness from the safety of Canada makes sense to me.

I write a note for my parents in case they return home before I do, and hide it in their bedroom.

Pawing through the maps in my father's office, I find one of Vermont that's only a few years old. I know we have a newer one. Maybe my parents have taken it and gone off on foot ahead of me. Why shouldn't they? If the police were after them, too . . . if they thought I was safe in Haiti . . . why shouldn't they have gone?

I check every drawer in my mother's office, in my father's office, in their bedroom, and in my own. I manage to gather fifty-seven dollars in stashed money. It feels as if I've struck gold.

In my backpack goes the Vermont map, a thermos, a spoon and fork, a flashlight, spare batteries, a pocket knife, three books of matches, a first aid kit, a length of rope, a roll of duct tape, an old blanket, a change of clothes, and

Jethro's bear. At the last moment I grab two handfuls of my mother's loose photographs and zip *them* into my pack too. Something to look at while I'm on the road, something to keep me from missing "home" too much.

Everything else I can live without.

———

Dressing in drab colors makes me nearly invisible. I plan on following Route 5 all the way north, along the eastern edge of the state. Route 5 should take me up to Newport, where, with any luck, I'll slip across the Canadian border as easily as I slipped into Vermont . . . quietly, unnoticed.

Once I'm safely away from the U.S. I'll figure out what comes next. No point in planning too far in advance.

In the last moments before leaving the house, I gather some of my most precious things and stow them in the crawl space in the attic for safekeeping.

I don't know what drives me to hide these things but I feel better after it's done.

———

Escaping into the night, I hesitate for a moment in my father's garden. A shape emerges from the house across the street.

I freeze. The person across the street freezes, too.

When I start again, I take long, soundless strides, resisting the urge to look behind me, prepared to fight if there's another attack.

At the corner I steal a quick glance over my shoulder. The person has stopped mid-block. He stands watching me. I don't fear him, there is no aggression in his posture. But I don't like that I've been seen.

I cross an empty Route 30, then hurry along the Common.

At last I turn north on Route 5.

When I look again, there is no one behind me.

Silently I say good-bye to my parents.

I tell them, *I can take care of myself. I can do this.*

But I don't know if I've ever been as homesick as I am at this moment, walking north in the dead of night, away from Brattleboro, away from home.

part two

Occasionally, a small group of people glides through an empty parking lot as I make my way out of town. We avoid each other.

I move quietly, on full alert.

It seems I have chosen a good night to leave. The moon is waxing full and makes it easier to see in the dark despite a thin cloud cover.

Those of us defying the curfew are so vulnerable. This part of Route 5 is just one long strip of commercial development, one parking lot after another. It's astounding that not a single car comes past.

Caution slows me. I am as wary as a cat. I imagine threats behind me and frequently spin to catch a would-be assailant only to find an empty road at my back.

———

The shops eventually give way to woods. The moon has gone behind a dense mat of clouds. It's impossible to have anything but a dim sense of where to put my feet. But I feel safer than I did walking through the parking lots. And each step north takes me farther from the law knocking at my door.

The night is long, punctuated by the occasional barking of dogs. But no one opens a door to look out. It is almost as if they're afraid to check what has startled their pets.

I remember a few years ago hearing about a pack of dogs that hunted at night just for the pleasure of the kill. They weren't hungry. They were well-cared-for pets. But they'd gotten a taste for blood, for the chase, slaughtering small livestock within an ever-broadening circle of their homes. People were afraid the pack would turn on children next.

I wonder if abandoned dogs are forming packs now, preying on solitary walkers.

Inside my head a voice whispers, *Don't think those things. Think about getting to Canada. Think about finding Mom and Dad. Don't think about anything else.*

———

At last, after hours of walking, I reach the village of Putney. The town is densely settled. I carefully thread my way through and continue north a little longer before crawling inside a shed and sitting out the remainder of the night.

Through this evening's entire march I saw no cars at all

and only one small convoy of military vehicles. And it was easy to hide from them.

Holding Jethro's bear, I huddle in the abandoned shed and imagine my parents just up ahead, encouraging me.

Knowing their preference for small roads, I think they, too, could easily be walking Route 5. They certainly drive it often enough. My mother's taken hundreds of pictures along this road.

The idea quickens my heart. The idea that I might find them.

———

With a couple hours of sleep to go on I resume my daytime schedule. I feel safest walking in daylight. I don't worry about packs of dogs. I worry about a thousand other things . . . what I'll eat, where I can wash up and relieve myself, whether I'll find a safe place to stop for the night, whether someone will get too curious about me, whether I'll make it all the way to Canada before I'm arrested, whether someone will hurt me, or kill me, whether I'll be hit by a car, whether I'll find my parents along the way . . . but I don't worry about packs of dogs.

I'm comforted by the number of people walking the road with me. Some heading north, some south. Though we avoid making eye contact, I feel less conspicuous with so many other walkers.

They're obviously not all heading to Canada. I don't know where they're going. I'm not about to ask.

Daytime traffic is pretty light compared with what it used to be. I guess because fuel has been so scarce. Nearly every service station I pass has a sign saying "No Gas." That may explain why my parents left on foot. It may also explain why there are so many others walking.

On this part of Route 5 the road is treacherous, twisting around corners with no shoulder to speak of, sharp, dented guardrails, and rock walls hovering over the road. I travel as deep into the shoulder as I can get, but there are times when there's no place to be safe.

Occasionally I get squeezed between a guardrail and a speeding car. Some drivers do their best to avoid me by drifting into the opposite lane, but some get a thrill out of terrifying me, coming as close as possible without hitting me.

Trucks are the worst, though. When they pass I'm slammed by a wall of wind that at best stings my skin but sometimes lifts me right off my feet.

Fortunately there are even fewer trucks on Route 5 than cars. And fewer cars than slow-moving military vehicles. And *they* don't seem to be interested in stopping along Route 5. At least so far.

I'm tired from walking through most of the night last night, through most of the day today. I'm ready to stop long before curfew but my search for collapsing barns, abandoned houses, unlocked sheds to slip inside for the night proves unsuccessful. I push myself to keep going. My burning eyes sweep over both sides of the road, desperate for a place to stop. And, at last, a sagging barn offers itself.

The night, though cool, is sweetly scented with blossom. I curl up inside my parents' old camping blanket and try to sleep. I'm dead tired. My legs ache, my mind is mostly a dull buzz. But there is this hot wire of alertness that never goes out and keeps me from sleeping truly deeply.

Another day, another section of road that curves and rolls unceasingly up, down, and around narrow shoulders where it is almost impossible to get out of the way of traffic. Fortunately, there's less and less traffic all the time, particularly on the long stretches of road between towns.

Trying to make my cash last, I've become expert at picking food out of Dumpsters . . . bar trash is the best. It turns out deep-fried potato skins covered in melted cheese

is my favorite. I never used to like that stuff . . . too greasy.
Now I fantasize about it.

A lot of restaurants seem to have closed, but the bars
appear to be doing fine. Most of them use generators. I can
hear the growl of the motor long before I reach it.

Trash pickup isn't regular either. Garbage cans over-
flow, Dumpsters are filled to the brim. It's easy pickings. I
just wish there were a few more of them.

I walk through Westminster, Bellows Falls, Springfield. I walk through woodland and farmland.

For long stretches I'm within view of the Connecticut River.

I follow trails into the woods from time to time where I can rest and eat, relieve myself, study the map. I still have so far to go. But I'm chuffed at how far I've come already.

Washing up in a gas station bathroom, I wish I had someone to walk with. Someone to talk with.

I miss the children at Paradis des Enfants more than I can say. Not even Jethro's bear comforts me. At least not enough.

I miss Chloe and the hours we spent cruising the neighborhoods with our hips swaying, sassing anyone who passed us. My hips aren't swaying now.

Small cuts, bruises, and bites lick their little tongues of fire all over me. Some jerk throws a soda can at my head out his open car window. I pick up the can after it hits me and cash it in for the deposit at a market in Ascutney.

As curfew approaches I take shelter behind an abandoned building. There is no roof over me tonight, but it's not raining and the bugs aren't bad.

My legs scream with pain after another long day's march.

I groan silently, easing myself down, trying to get comfortable.

Until I turned thirteen, I hiked with my parents every Sunday morning. I loved those hikes. I can admit it now.

I miss walking with my father, stopping to examine a plant, learning its Latin name. I miss my mother, obsessively recording with her camera the fall of light through leaves, the growth of fungi on trees, a rock cairn left by hikers who came before.

If only I knew which way my parents had gone. It's possible they were arrested and are sitting in some jail now. But I choose to believe, instead, that they, too, are making their way to Canada.

They would advise, "Radley, keep yourself safe. We'll find you when this nightmare is over."

I'm hopeful I'll find them before that.

I must not allow even a moment's lapse in attention. Not a moment. Less than an hour ago the police caught someone who was heading toward the woods where I had only just hidden. The siren screamed, the revolving light making terrifying shadows in the trees and across the sky.

I'd only been in here a few minutes. Only just wrapped myself in my parents' camp blanket. If I'd tried to squeeze in one more mile, tried to find a place that felt safer, a barn, a shed, if I hadn't given up exactly when I did and settled for sleeping under the trees, the police would have caught *me*.

If the traveler had not been caught, he would have spent the night in these woods so close to me I don't know how I could have avoided him. With so many of us on the road, why hasn't this happened before, why hasn't someone else ducked into the same place I'm hiding for the night?

Or maybe it has happened. Maybe I have spent the night in a barn where someone else lay hidden, someone who felt safer remaining concealed from me.

I pull my knees up under my chin and don't realize I'm crying until I wipe away the tickling on my cheek and my hand comes away wet.

Today the walking is miserable, in heavy rain.

My mom loves rain walking. She'd come back from hours of following wet paths, her hair and coat dripping.

She'd stand in the front hall making puddles on the floor.

I wrinkled my nose at the scent she carried up the stairs with her on those days. That wet wool smell.

How I took for granted being warm and dry.

Mom would come into my room, having stripped out of her wet things, her robe belted around her waist, and she'd sit on the side of my bed with her animal eyes and her damp hair smelling like dog fur.

I loathe walking in the rain.

I'm chilled and drenched and wretched.

When I find an empty house somewhere south of Windsor with a For Sale sign in front, I consider my options. The house has a deep, concealing porch. The grass on the lawn is up past my knees. If I climb onto that porch I'll be invisible from the road.

If a realtor comes to show someone the place . . . I can get away . . . I make a quick plan of how to escape if a car pulls into the driveway. And then I'm up on the porch and hunkering down before I can change my mind.

I spend the day under the shelter of that porch roof. This is the first day I've allowed myself to stop. I'm torn, thinking I can catch up with my parents if I just keep going. But today the need to find my parents is not as strong as my need for shelter.

Maybe my parents are doing the same. Mom likes walking in the rain, but Dad hates it as much as I do. Maybe they are just up ahead, sitting knee to knee in an abandoned horse stall, congratulating each other again on how smart they were to send me to Haiti when they did.

Another day of drenching rain.

After spending the night on the porch, I'm tempted to stay but I'm afraid of stopping any place for too long.

I climb down off the porch and walk through Windsor, instantly regretting my decision to keep moving. Rain slides its chill fingers through my hair, down my collar. I am so cold, so wet.

My hair hangs dripping over my face. I must look like

something the cat dragged in. I definitely feel like something the cat dragged in.

After raiding a moderately satisfying Dumpster (no potato skins, no French fries, but an end of salami and some burnt chili in a soggy cardboard tub), I look again for a place of refuge.

Settling inside an empty barn, I remember one time, several years ago, my mother brought a package in from the front porch and carried it up the stairs to my bedroom.

"For you," she said. "From Grammy."

My mother's mother had stunning taste. But she had no idea who I was or what I liked. Her gift to me was a cowgirl dress, a jaundice-yellow fabric printed with brown horses. It was the ugliest dress I'd ever seen. I couldn't bring myself to put it on. I couldn't imagine wearing it, even as a joke.

I feel a deep pain, like a punch to the gut.

I'd wear it now, if only I could have my parents, my grandparents, my old life back.

I'd wear it now.

Did I do the right thing leaving home? I'm so tired. I don't know how I can keep going. The weather feels more like March than June. My skin is wet rubber.

The route twists and turns, heading south when I want to go north, east when I need to go west. I know I'm making progress. But I still have so far to go. And my map is coming to pieces in this sodden weather.

If I surrendered quietly, at least I would have shelter and food. And I could dry out.

Occasionally I find a dripping newspaper in a trash bin. Most of it falls apart as I try to turn the pages but there are articles about snipers picking off soldiers. Farmers protecting their property with hunting rifles. Prisons overflowing with looters and protestors. Under this emergency law, anything can get you arrested.

I feel cut loose from the world.

I wonder if the world actually still exists.

I'm floating in some alien universe without an air supply.

And I'm drowning in all this rain.

The sun finally breaks through late in the afternoon. I
unfold my damp, gray, stiff, miserable body and begin
to walk again.

I think about the children of Haiti, how they welcomed
me, arms open, pushing their small bodies up against mine
for the sweetness of human contact. I understand now. I
understand hunger for the touch of another. I step off the

road into the woods, look at the shredded map for the hundredth time, and lift up my face as the rain of the last few days evaporates from my hair, my boots, my skin; threads of steam rise off my clothes toward the warming sun.

I think of the children at Paradis des Enfants and hope they have not had so much rain.

White River Junction crawls with soldiers.

I'm terrified they'll notice me. I try in every way to avoid calling attention to myself.

They have nothing to fear from me. They never did. I don't want to topple a government.

I only want to be dry and safe, I only want something hot to eat.

I only want to find my parents and get my old life back.

My head itches, my hair stinks. I don't bother letting it out of its clip. It's too disgusting. Why didn't I cut it before I left? I'd do it now if I had a pair of scissors bigger than the snips in my first aid kit. Of course if I chopped all my hair off I'd be more conspicuous. But it feels as if my scalp is crawling with vermin.

Once, when I visited my cousin in Montreal, I spent a small fortune to have my hair cut. My cousin had been teasing me about being a country mouse. In that beautiful city, in my flannel shirt and jeans, I *felt* like a country mouse. And so my cousin took me to her hair salon and I didn't ask the cost.

My father paled when he got the bill. But he swallowed

hard and told me my hair looked beautiful. All he said was he hoped my haircut would keep its shape for a very long time.

Once again I'm going to Canada dressed like a clod. And once again I'm in need of a haircut. I'd head for Montreal straightaway if my cousin was still there. But she lives in Miami now. At least she lived in Miami before all of this began.

I'm careful. Kids congregate in out-of-the-way places . . . the sort of places I seek for shelter. They look restless, angry, short fused. Usually they cluster in groups of threes and fives. The looks they give me are dangerous. I could never stand alone against them. It is safer to back away, not test them, even if they are close to my age. I can tell where I'm not wanted. Where I'm not safe.

So I'm surprised when not everyone looks at me with suspicion. A small boy waves to me as I pass. A little girl wearing butterfly wings and clinging to her mother's hand turns and smiles at me over her shoulder. These fleeting moments of kindness give me hope that the world is not completely lost. I replay them in my head as I walk, as I settle down for the night. Like Jethro's bear, they comfort and console me.

Several times I have seen bikes and considered stealing one. But stealing a bike is not like stealing those quarters from the people at the Manchester airport.

What a difference a bike would make. How many more miles I could cover in a day. How much more normal I

would appear, pedaling a bike along the empty stretches of
Route 5.

But I can't steal someone's bike.

And besides, I never learned to ride one.

There is a girl I've caught sight of several times. I'm curious about her.

How much I miss human contact. My mother was always hugging me, kissing my cheeks, brushing my hair off my forehead. It used to drive me crazy. I'd snap at her, try to hurt her, to keep her at a distance. Why did I do that? Why?

I fear this girl. She looks defiant, something in the way she holds her bony shoulders as she walks, something fierce in the glimpses I get of her pale face. And she travels with a dog. Just the sort of dog that has always frightened me. When I was little, the same sort of dog jumped on me, knocked me over. It terrified me. I don't want to get too close to either of them.

I follow behind, silently, keeping a healthy distance.

But as wary as I am of the two of them, I also feel strangely drawn to them. The girl doesn't look like the children at the orphanage, but there is something about her.

I creep along rather than stretching my legs at full stride. The girl moves slowly, as if something hurts inside her.

We stop for rest, food, water at matched intervals. The synchronization of wayfarers.

If the girl gets ahead it's easy to catch up to her.

I worry about this attachment I'm forming. My mind wanders, spinning fantasies about her. It's pure relief to think of something other than myself for a change. But it's dangerous to let myself become so distracted. I realize a police car has driven past me several times in the last hour. I pray he's not looking for me and take the first opportunity to duck into a gas station, get myself off the road, try to make myself look a little less travel worn.

And then, a mile or so later, I'm nearly creamed by the same cop as he comes careening around a blind corner, siren screaming. His car comes close enough, it brushes my sleeve.

Almost being hit steals my breath away. Makes my heart thunder. But there is also relief. He is after someone else.

The girl and her dog stepped off the road and into the woods moments before the policeman skimmed past me. They did not emerge from the trees after the tail lights disappeared.

Fine. I take the lead. Force myself not to look into the woods when I pass the place where she vanished. I just keep walking.

The weather turns foul again this morning. I find another empty house, another protected porch. With some food and water in my pack, I decide to wait out the rain.

I think maybe I've been dozing. Suddenly, a dog stands over me.

The fuzziness of sleep instantly vanishes. Replaced by the sharp focus of fear.

Pressing my back against the porch wall, I try inching away but the dog keeps closing the distance between us.

I jerk myself to a standing position, surprised when the dog shows no sign of aggression at my sudden move.

Instead, the dog lowers itself to its belly and inches close enough I can feel a trace of heat coming off it. Then it raises its nose and touches the hem of my pants. So gently.

It rolls onto its back and whines.

Even I can see the dog is submitting to me. But it is the girl's dog. At least it looks exactly like the girl's dog, the girl I'd been following.

The dog rolls back over, rises slowly, bows to me. It whines. Climbs off the porch, looks back at me, waits for me to follow.

I don't know why I decide to go with it. Except, that girl. There is something about that girl.

Checking first to make certain no one is watching, with my blanket still wrapped around my shoulders, I grab my pack and step down from the protection of the porch, into the torrential rain.

The dog trots a few steps ahead, then turns to note my progress.

I had almost dried out on the porch. Now I'm instantly soaked again. I consider going back, but I don't think I have that option anymore.

I think the dog is determined to retrieve me.

I'm led behind an abandoned silo where the girl is nearly hidden in the undergrowth. She's deathly pale except for a blaze of red on each cheek. I touch her forehead. Fever ravages her.

Speaking gently, I cover the girl with my blanket, though it is already soaked and offers her no protection from the rain. I lift her head slightly and put my thermos of water to her lips. Her eyes flutter open, register my presence, then close again.

I have the money I collected from my parents' drawers. I've been saving it. But I don't hesitate to spend it now. Just as I used my money in Haiti to feed the children when they told me their stomachs hurt, now I must use what I have to save this girl's life.

"My name is Radley," I tell her. "Your dog brought me here. I think you need food. And water. I'm going to get something to help you feel better. I'll be right back." I don't know how much she's heard but she nods and groans. The dog lies down beside her, its head on its paws.

I remember passing a market in Norwich. I walk back to it, buy some Gatorade. I stop in at a little café and ask for some plain cooked rice, waiting while they fix it for me. When I ask how much I owe, the owner waves me away, tells me to feel better. I head back to the girl, almost expecting her to have vanished but she's still there, shivering under my sodden blanket.

I give her sips of the Gatorade.

With each ounce of fluid, she claws her way out from the pit.

We are exposed in a way that makes me nervous. We have only the leaves overhead as protection from the rain. But I don't dare move her.

The dog never leaves us for more than a few minutes and I realize I feel safe and useful in a way I have not felt since Haiti.

Within twenty-four hours the girl seems much better. "My name's Celia," she croaks. "My dog is Jerry Lee."

"You heading north?" I ask.

Celia shrugs and says nothing more.

When she's well enough to travel again we begin walking together. Celia makes it clear she doesn't want to talk.

I think she's too depleted, too exhausted to do anything but put one foot in front of the other.

I try to hold my tongue but there are so many questions I want to ask.

As it is, we don't cover much ground our first day walking together.

After we've settled down in the woods for the night, I try again to question her. Rudely, she turns her back to me and goes to sleep.

I yearn to hear the sound of my own voice, to hear the sound of hers. I've been alone for so long. After the intimacy of the children at the orphanage, I ache for someone beside me.

At the end of our second day of silence Celia tersely thanks me for nursing her back to health.

I use the small opening she's given me to ask where she started her journey.

But she doesn't respond.

What if she decides to flag down a cop? What if she turns me over to one of the convoys of soldiers passing on the road? I don't know anything about her.

But I hate the idea of being alone again. I decide to keep trying with her, at least a little longer.

"Are you still in school?" I ask.

She glares at me for a moment. Doesn't answer.

I decide to ignore her rudeness. I imagine, instead, an orphan at my side, holding my hand, singing in a high, sweet voice.

It doesn't help.

Celia prefers to sleep in the woods. I prefer sheds and barns.

Grudgingly, after a brief exchange, she agrees to decide at the end of each day whether we can slip, undetected, into some sort of shelter or whether we are better off under the trees.

When no shelter presents itself at the close of day, we have little choice but to stay in the woods. Jerry Lee is the most agreeable of the three of us. He sleeps wherever Celia sleeps, no protests, no questions asked.

One evening, behind a condemned house, in a sagging barn hidden from the road, Celia gazes out at the rain slamming down through the darkness and admits the night's accommodation, under a roof, leaky as it is, has some advantage. Water runs down the walls and collects in puddles, but we are able to find a dry stall to share with the mice and the mosquitoes and the ghosts of horses past.

Once we're beyond Lyndon, areas of settlement thin out even more. We are about two-thirds of the way now. I've spent most of my money on food . . . Celia is much fussier about Dumpster diving, though once I get her started, she can't resist raiding the trash bins behind Dunkin' Donuts.

The power supply is so erratic. One night we'll see lights in farmhouses as evening approaches but the next evening everything is dark again. Gas must still be scarce, too, judging by the lack of cars on the road. There are fewer walkers this far north. But enough that we don't stand out.

Following a brief discussion, we agree to spend the night in an old barn in an overgrown field. The sun has been down for a couple of hours when we hear the sound of feet approaching. Jerry Lee is up instantly, making a noise in his throat I've never heard before.

Outside, it sounds like a mob on the move. The ground shakes with their approach.

I think, now we are going to die. Why didn't I listen to Celia about not sheltering in barns?

Jerry Lee seems to be considering our options. He puts his nose under Celia's hand, and indicates his intention to leave. Silently we gather our things, silently we begin to move toward the back of the barn. Making his way in the dark, Jerry Lee guides us through a low door. We crawl out into an overgrown yard while a mass of boys push on the side of the barn, intent on collapsing it. Slithering across the weedy expanse, we slowly make our way to the woods beyond.

The weary barn groans in protest as the boys continue pushing on it. They grow louder with their effort and their excitement.

I tremble with fear in our hiding place inside a thicket of trees. Jerry Lee leans against me, comfortingly.

As part of the barn tilts impossibly, sighs, and collapses, headlights come down the road, shining on the young mob. The boys scatter.

One runs into the woods not far from where we are hiding. He passes so close we can hear his breath.

He exits again at a distance, never seeing us.

The rest of the barn lets go on its own and the dust makes us sneeze, though we make no sound. Our eyes burn and tear.

The police search through the rubble for hours, and then, satisfied there's no more to be done, they leave.

Their headlights disappear around the bend. The sound of their tires trails off into the distance.

Celia whispers, "About a month ago kids started setting fire to barns, but one of the fires spread and took out two cornfields and a house. Now the little thugs just push stuff over. They're trying to scare anyone hiding inside."

"It worked," I say. "I thought we were going to die. I'm sorry, Celia. I didn't know about any of this."

"It's not your fault," Celia says, thawing a bit. "I should have told you why I didn't want to spend the night in a barn."

I kneel in the underbrush and wrap my arms around Jerry Lee. "Thank you," I whisper into his fur. He suffers my embrace.

When I let him go, he moves away, sits beside Celia, gazing into what's left of the night.

We say no more about it. But from then on, Celia decides where we stop to sleep.

Route 5 has pulled away from the Connecticut River and I miss it. The river had been my steady companion for so many miles of this journey. It provided a place of rest and welcome.

Now acres of farmland alternate with miles and miles of woods.

Having Jerry Lee along makes us look almost normal, like a couple of girls out walking the dog.

I travel the slow swing of Jerry Lee's and Celia's gait, my eyes always scanning the horizon for my parents. If only Jerry Lee could find them somewhere along this road . . .

But how many miracles is one dog allowed?

Celia begins to relax with me. When a girl comes tearing past in a red convertible, Celia looks at me and says, "Sweet."

I tell Celia, "My friend Chloe had a convertible. Well, it was her father's really. A Corvette. It was his pride and joy. He didn't let anyone touch it. But once Chloe picked me up in it and we cruised down to Massachusetts and back. Her father tried to punish her when she brought the 'Vette home, but it was hard to punish Chloe."

Celia doesn't make a comment, but she doesn't turn away either.

Having Celia turn to me and say "sweet," it's like she's given me a gift.

Telling her about Chloe, I am giving her one, too, whether she knows it or not.

Celia grumbles about the endless miles, but for me they
begin to fall away.

I've hit some sort of stride. My body no longer minds
the endless foot pounding, the discomfort of nights spent

on hard ground or inside abandoned barns. I no longer expect every car to hit me, I no longer expect every cop to arrest me. Having Celia and Jerry Lee at my side gives me something to think about.

In Barton a man pulls up alongside us. He smiles at us through his open car window. He's got a nice face. A warm smile. He warns us to be careful, that there are people around looking to hurt us. He says if we want we can spend the night at his place; that tomorrow he'll give us a ride wherever we need to go. Meanwhile we can have a hot shower, eat some real food, sleep in a soft bed.

It's the first time anyone has approached this way in all the weeks I've been walking. I never thought there might be safe houses, but that's what he's offering. I wonder whether Celia and Jerry Lee and I look so obviously out of place here, or whether this guy is particularly perceptive.

I tell him thanks and start to move toward his car when Celia grabs my hand and stops me. Her eyes flit over to Jerry Lee.

His hackles are up.

Celia, squeezing my hand, tells the man our aunt is waiting for us, that we're staying with her for the summer, that we have to get back soon or we'll be in big trouble.

It's the most I've heard Celia say since we started walking together.

"I could drive you there," he offers. "To your aunt's . . ."

I don't understand why Celia and Jerry Lee have taken against him. He's so accommodating. And what he offers is so tempting. Surely he's someone we could trust. Wouldn't I sense it if he weren't?

But I decide to remain with Celia and Jerry Lee anyway.

"Sorry," I apologize to the guy, genuinely embarrassed. "But thanks anyway."

Suddenly the guy transforms. His expression turns ugly. He spits at us.

"Stupid bitches," he snarls. Then he peels away.

I stare after him, totally shocked. "What a jerk! What a freakin' jerk! How did you know?" I asked. "How did Jerry Lee know?"

"It's a skill we've developed," Celia says.

"Thanks," I say. "I would have gone with him."

She nods. "Good thing you didn't. Guess we're even now."

"Even?" I ask.

"You saved my life. I've just saved yours."

We are close to the border. I worry about that creep coming back for us. I worry about crossing into Canada. So we switch our waking and sleeping, waiting for full darkness before starting out.

Used to be I fretted most about the curves in the road and someone coming around the corner too fast and hitting me. *Now* the scariest sections are the ones where we can see for a distance in every direction. If *we* can see that far, everyone can see us, too.

But up here, as we approach the Canadian border, there's almost no traffic and very few walkers.

Each night the natural light has lingered a little longer, the darkness closing in a bit later. I'm not sure of the exact date though I wonder if we're near the solstice. That would make sense.

When I left Brattleboro, I walked out of town under a waxing moon. Tonight the dark is nearly impenetrable.

Celia and I walk haltingly, each of us with a hand in contact with Jerry Lee, moving blindly, closer and closer to the Canadian border. When a car approaches we drop down. There's almost always a place to get off the road.

But there are almost never any cars.

"I wonder how long the power will be out this time," I whisper.

Celia shrugs. "It's been like this for a long time now. On one night, off three. Hackers, probably."

"There've got to be people clever enough to counter the hackers," I say.

Celia laughs quietly. "Sure there are. But they were some of the first to be picked up and hauled off to jail."

Finally we make it to Newport.

After all of this walking at last we've reached the border. We move silently through the sleeping town.

"Tonight we cross," I whisper.

Celia nods. I feel it more than see it.

"I never asked if you had a passport," I say.

Celia is silent for a few moments. "Do I look like I have a passport?" she answers.

I shake my head no, which, of course, she can't see.

"You do, don't you?" Celia says.

"Yes," I say. "Yes, I have a passport."

"Why the hell don't you just go through a legal crossing then?" she snaps.

"I can't."

All this time I've wanted to share stories with her but now . . .

"It better not be because you feel sorry for me," Celia says in a low growl.

"It's got nothing to do with you, Celia," I say. "The police are after me."

"Oh," she says finally.

By now it's past midnight. Everything is still but for a night bird out on the lake.

I walk close to Celia as if we're old friends on a lark, as if she's Chloe and we're in the middle of another crazy adventure. Jerry Lee looks up at us, surprised.

"We are just two friends from Newport, out after curfew. Two restless girls and a dog," I say, and Celia leans into me.

We follow the narrow road along the western shore of Lake Memphremagog. But before we get to where the road ends I stop, the hairs rising on my neck. There's a white car about a quarter mile ahead of us, parked in the road.

I take Celia's hand and guide her down a hill, behind a shed. "I think there's someone in that car."

"It's just parked there," Celia whispers.

"Humor me," I urge.

"For how long? We're so close, Radley."

"How much would it suck if we get picked up now, Celia, within sight of Canada?"

Celia sighs, sits down with her back against the shed, and pats the ground for Jerry Lee. But Jerry Lee remains standing at attention beside me.

We watch for only a minute or two, and then, slowly, silently, the white car begins moving. An industrial-strength flashlight pans across the fields on either side of the road, as if the driver thinks he's seen something. The beam probes the perimeters of the shed, but we are well hidden. Still my heart thunders. The car moves particularly slowly as it comes parallel with us.

But it keeps going, heading away from the border, back in the direction of town.

As soon as the tail lights vanish, we tear up onto the road and this time we are running.

In moments we arrive at a metal guardrail.

It's clear we're meant to stop.

But we don't stop. We keep going.

Climbing over the rail on the American side, we blaze through a swath of underbrush to another rail thirty feet away.

And just like that, we're over the border.

We are exhilarated, continuing on pure adrenaline. We pass a farm occasionally as we move deeper and deeper into Canada. Mostly, we are flanked by dense trees.

"We should get some sleep," I say at last, stumbling over my own feet.

Celia nods and a few minutes later she and Jerry Lee lead the way into the woods. Her instincts are good. She finds us a comfortable patch of ground to spend the rest of the night.

We begin traveling by day again.

I've been wondering what would happen once we crossed but I've been afraid to ask. Not that Celia would have answered.

But I try now. "Do you want to stay together now that we're over?"

She nods. It's the closest we've come to friendship. But I'm afraid to push her. I'm learning to be quiet.

Stopping at a brook, we kneel and drink.

"Why are the police after you?" she asks.

"I don't know. Something to do with my parents, I think. They've been really public about their opposition to the American People's Party from the start."

Celia nods.

"What about you?" I ask. "Why are you running?"

Celia shrugs.

And that's all I get.

We have no plan.

We simply move together for another week, heading west and north.

All the signs are in French. Celia relies entirely on my translations.

When the road we're fol-
lowing ends, we begin
to blaze a path through dense
forest.

Celia sets the pace and we
continue slowly, over rugged
terrain, for another two days,
eating what I have left in my
backpack, until we reach an
abandoned place deep in the
woods.

There's an old sign over
the front door. "School of
Hope," it says.

"Home sweet home," Celia
declares.

"I'm not sure about this,
Celia."

But Celia is sure.

She's finished walking.

The paint, where there is paint on the school's exterior, is chipped and dulled to a dirty gray. Several mismatched windows reveal stained shreds of curtain. No stack for plumbing, no chimney for a stove. I think this is what realtors call "rustic."

The glass in one of the windows is missing. I approach cautiously and peer inside.

"No one here," I announce. "Probably hasn't been for a long time."

"Shocking," Celia says softly.

I ignore her sarcasm. "I think we can get in through a window."

But Celia lifts a rock from the ground. I think she's going to use it to break more glass, but she studies it instead, puts it back down and picks up another. She lowers the second rock and after scanning the ground with her eyes, she begins to explore the level surfaces of the schoolhouse.

"Hah!" She sounds quietly triumphant. Jerry Lee's tail wags.

Celia holds up a key she's found on a ledge above a window.

The lock is stiff and it takes some effort but the key eventually turns and the door opens.

Rodents and birds have been the sole students at this school for some time. It smells foul. Dried animal droppings litter every surface. We have nothing to sweep with, nothing to scrub with. Still, using what the surrounding woods offer, boughs, and leaves, and brook water, using our ingenuity, we begin to bring order.

The entire structure consists of two rooms, each about

ten feet by twelve. One of the rooms contains a rusted metal bed frame with a stained piece of plywood suspended on the narrow rim where a box spring and mattress might go. The mattress and springs are gone, but I am so grateful for this bed frame, dismal as it is, set at an angle in the middle of the floor of an old country schoolhouse.

Celia and I hardly talk.

We just work together, making the abandoned schoolhouse habitable.

By the end of the day the outside looks unchanged.

But inside, a sanctuary emerges. I gather armfuls of fresh grass and cattails from nearby. We pile them inside the metal frame on top of the plywood and I spread my old blanket over, tucking it in on all four sides.

When the sun sets, wordlessly we agree to share the bed. We sink down, grass spilling over the sides. The blanket emits an almost human sigh beneath us.

I am so hungry. Our bed makes me long for green salad.

And my fingers itch for Jethro's bear, nestled inside my backpack. But the bear hasn't been out since Celia and I started traveling together.

Unable to fall asleep, I grieve for my empty hands.

I grieve for not finding my parents on the way to Canada.

I grieve, worrying I may never find them again.

Celia, still on our makeshift bed, sits up and inhales the fresh air wafting through the open door. The schoolhouse, on this sunlit morning, has begun to take on the scent of girls with wind-blown hair, with seeds in their pockets, with road-hardened feet.

"I've got food," I say and empty my backpack of the bits I've gathered from several kitchen gardens: baby lettuce, baby peas, baby radishes.

We devour the tiny pile of food.

"When did you have time . . . ?"

"I went out early, while it was still dark."

Celia's wild, thick hair strains to free itself from the rubber band confining it. "Who would build a school out here in the middle of nowhere?" she asks, nibbling a small, peppery radish.

"We're not as far off the beaten track as you think," I say. "Once you get out beyond these woods it's small farms, some houses, a little town called Sutton. Maybe, a long time ago, kids followed a path to school here, but there are no paths leading here now."

And if we're to remain hidden and safe, we'll have to keep it that way.

Hunger drives me out of bed each morning, hours before dawn. I explore the area while Celia sleeps. She has no interest in coming out with me. Or even in going out on her own.

Celia says she's walked enough. She's not taking another step.

From all appearances the Canadian government remains stable despite the chaos in the U.S. But Celia and I are here illegally. Even with my passport I would be thrown out of this country. I've crossed the border without asking permission, I'm here for an indefinite period, and I'm wanted by the police in my own country.

It feels safest to keep as low a profile as possible, traveling a different route each day.

This early in the season, the vegetable gardens are barely

producing. I make my way to Sutton, instead, and creep up to a Dumpster behind a small café.

A woman, about ten years younger than my mother, surprises me in the act of lifting the Dumpster lid. She has padded up behind me so silently.

I freeze, certain she will turn me over to the Canadian police.

When I open my mouth to plead for her silence, she holds up a hand, a gesture that signals me to wait, and she flies back through the rear door of the restaurant.

I have no idea what she wants but I can't risk finding out. I flee the moment she turns her back on me and run from Sutton empty-handed.

Consequently, Celia and I have little to eat the rest of the day.

I think about using what few coins remain of my money to buy food, but it's American currency. It would give us away instantly.

Celia is so pale; she seems to grow thinner each day. I feel like I'm responsible for her and that scares me. In the past, I've blown it big-time when it comes to being responsible. I always screw up. Until now my parents have bailed me out, made things right again, as right as they could. But my parents aren't here now.

And somebody has to keep Celia alive.

I'll do what I can.

For days I'm afraid to return to Sutton, afraid to venture out at all, afraid the woman from the restaurant has reported me. That the Canadian police are watching for me.

I plunder a garden not far from the schoolhouse. The

vegetable plot sits like a small brown package in a field of green grass. Moving through the young lettuce and onion plants, I take only a handful of greens, then slip inside the barn searching for anything else.

I find root vegetables left over from last year and "borrow" a dented pail to carry back to the schoolhouse the lettuce and onion greens, four withered potatoes, and six soft carrots.

Celia eagerly falls on the carrots. We make a meal out of raw, desiccated vegetables, and fresh lettuce and onion tops.

"Why aren't you with your parents?" Celia asks.

I tell her we were separated. That I was out of town when all this started. I'm not sure why I'm afraid to tell her the truth, to tell her I was in Haiti. I think maybe she won't approve. Maybe it makes me sound too rich, too spoiled. I don't know what made me think I could help down there, anyway. I bathed dusty toddlers in plastic buckets. I braided thick hair and buttoned thin shirts. I spooned cornmeal mush into bowls. I did what I could. But the kids did ten times for me what I did for them.

Celia gnaws on a raw, soft potato. When I ask her why she isn't with her parents, she shrugs and keeps gnawing.

I'm getting to know those shrugs pretty well. And the uneasy silence that follows them.

I offer a potato to Jerry Lee. With one sniff he refuses my generosity, asking to be let out instead, where he chases down his own food.

I roam the countryside alone. Celia never comes.

She has no idea where I go. She just knows when she wakes, there'll be food waiting.

Though I'd like his company, Jerry Lee never leaves Celia's side. Except to eat. The only time he ever left her

was the time he retrieved me from the porch and got me to follow him into the woods. And he only did it then to save Celia's life.

Several days in a row I fail to find enough food to satisfy us. Celia has trouble holding down the little I do manage to bring.

Even Jerry Lee doesn't seem to be eating enough.

I want to go back to the Dumpsters in Sutton. It's the way I've learned to survive. But Canada will surely deport me if I'm discovered. And then Celia would be left alone, not knowing where I am.

My feet bring me back instead to the farm where I found the withered carrots.

To my surprise, instead of police, what awaits me in the barn, in the place where I found (and stole) the dented pail, is a bar of soap, two men's button-down shirts, a pair of overalls, a pair of green trousers, and a paper bag filled with pods of fragrant green peas.

The clothes are worn and patched. But they're clean. I gather them into my arms and the smell of fresh laundry gives rise to a wave of homesickness. I stand in the barn, frozen for a moment, aching for my mother.

Is it possible these have been waiting for me? Is it possible someone is trying to help?

Quickly, I gather the clothes, the soap, the peas and head back to the schoolhouse before sunrise.

Celia sleeps deeply.

I shake her shoulder. "Look what we've got."

She's startled by the sudden wakening and swats at me.

After swearing for a minute, Celia pulls herself together.

She is amazed at what I've brought.

We hold the clothes up to ourselves. They won't fit either of us but it doesn't matter. We'll make them work.

"I'm using the soap before I put on new clothes," I say.

I draw Celia far enough from the schoolhouse to wash in the cold, clear brook that runs nearby. We put on our fresh things. Then sit on the schoolhouse step in the June sunshine, drying off, warming up, side by side.

"Celia, if I don't come back some day . . ."

"You'll come back."

"But if I don't, it's because I've been caught . . ."

"I know," Celia says.

"Will you be able to manage?"

Celia looks up at the sky. She nudges me with her bony shoulder. "You'll come back."

"But if I don't?"

Celia gets up and disappears inside the schoolhouse with Jerry Lee.

Conversation over.

W hat are you thinking about?" Celia asks later, sitting down beside me on the edge of our bed.

She's feeling better now that she's washed, in clean clothes, with a little food in her.

I'm thinking about my parents and their packages to Haiti. How the boxes arrived filled with clothes, food, crayons, workbooks. I'd call home the moment the boxes came and let my parents listen to the sound of the children opening them. It delighted my mom to know that of all the gifts she and Dad sent, the children loved her photographs the most, especially the ones of our cat, Romulus. She'd write these comical notes on the back in her very silly French, like "*Bonjour, ma petite souris. Je voudrais a manger votre queues*," as if Rom were calling the children his little mice and telling them he'd like to eat their tails.

"I'm thinking about my mom," I say. "She's a photographer."

"Is that what those pictures are?" Celia asks.

I nod. "Ever hear of Parker Hughes? She's kind of famous."

Most people get pretty excited when they find out who my mother is. But not Celia.

"What kind of name is Parker?" Celia asks.

"What kind of name is Radley?" I answer.

"Good point. Anyway, your mother's pictures are good," Celia says. "I like the ones of food . . ."

"Wait a minute. How do you even know about the photographs . . ."

"I've seen you looking at them. I was curious," Celia says. "I went through your pack. I like the bear, too."

I feel a black fury descend. "I would never go through your things . . ."

"I know," Celia says. And shrugs. "Anyway, your mom's pictures, they're really good."

I want to smack her. I want to scream at her. I want to go to my room and slam the door in her face.

And then I look at the tiny two-room schoolhouse and the possibility that it might all collapse with the slam of a door.

And I start to laugh.

"My mom made the bear. Knitting's a hobby of hers.

She says it calms her. But the bear's not mine. It's just on loan from a friend."

"I wouldn't mind borrowing it myself from time to time," Celia says. "Actually, I already have."

I'm torn between feeling really pissed at her for touching my things, and moved by the fact that she's drawn comfort from them.

"I would have thought you were too old for dolls," I finally manage to say.

"Yeah, I can see how you'd think that."

"How old *are* you?" I ask.

"Nineteen. I'll be twenty this summer. You?"

"Seventeen. Just a baby."

"Just a baby," Celia echoes.

I look to see if there is any meanness in her eyes and am surprised by the tears there instead. She turns away, gets up, and goes to the door to let out Jerry Lee.

Seeing the way Celia sleeps so deeply in our grass and cattail bed, seeing Jerry Lee look less and less wary when he hears anything moving outside in the woods, my own caution begins to subside.

Instinct tells us we have found a safe haven here, in Canada, under the shadow of the rugged mountains of southeastern Quebec. Is it possible my parents have found safety here, too? That in my wanderings I'll find them or hear of them?

There's not always food waiting for me at the farm nearby, but there's always something. Our Lady of the Barn is reliable in her care though she doesn't always know what we need.

What we need most is food, every day. We need food.

I am resentful on the days when no food is left for us. How quickly I revert to the spoiled child I was at home when my mother prepared every meal. On the days when Our Lady of the Barn doesn't come through with nourishment, I have to hustle to find enough to eat, often risking a heart-pounding race in and out of Sutton.

Sometimes I arrive too late to raid the trash there.

Observing from a hiding place, I notice how all the people on the streets of Sutton seem to know each other. I eavesdrop on their conversations. They're so relaxed. Not a soldier, not a cop in sight. It's so different from what I left behind in Vermont.

But these people would take note of a stranger in town, particularly one who came only to raid their garbage.

I am neither brave enough nor stupid enough to risk stealing food from Sutton in broad daylight.

But today there is no need. Today Our Lady of the Barn has been more than generous.

I find a pail of ripe strawberries.

A soft blanket.

A pair of shears.

"Thank you, O Lady of the Barn," I whisper, gathering her gifts. "Thank you!"

As I slip through the approaching dawn I look toward the house, trying to make out the figure of our benefactress. But there is no hint of her.

After Celia and I have eaten the strawberries, tossing three to Jerry Lee and watching him leap and snap the ripe red orbs out of the air, the sun is well up. With the pair of shears, Celia and I give each other haircuts out on the step of the schoolhouse. The breeze takes our locks scudding away amid the tall grasses and weeds.

We head down to the brook, and using the soap, we shampoo the stubble that is left on our heads.

Celia is better at cutting hair. Back at the schoolhouse, when I look at my reflection in the bowl of my spoon I am a pixie-headed stranger.

Celia does not complain but she looks as if I've cut her hair with an eggbeater.

"It's not your fault," she says. "It's my hair. It has a mind of its own." She rolls her eyes and we laugh.

At last we are free of all that weight, of its smell, of its itch.

Along with the hair, the rest of our reserve falls away.

I don't have to ask. Celia simply starts talking. My starved ears savor her every word. My brain, at full attention, memorizes each thing she says, each story she tells. It's as if she's heard my questions all along. Now she's finally ready to answer them.

"I've got two half-sisters back in Windsor," Celia says. "I had a brother, but he died."

"Your parents?"

Celia shakes her head no. Her chin juts out, a little gesture of defiance or self-control . . . I'm not sure which.

She stretches as if dislodging some memory. "How about you?" she asks. "Sisters? Brothers?"

"Only child," I say. "It's good. You don't have to share."

"Sharing was never the problem," Celia says.

"What was the problem?" I ask.

Celia raises her eyebrows. "Not remembering my father. Having a drunk mother. Then having no mother at all."

"Sorry," I say.

Celia shrugs. "Stuff happens."

But stuff like that never happened to me.

When there is no food waiting in Our Lady's barn, when I am too late to slip safely in and out of Sutton, I forage for food in the woods near the schoolhouse. I never manage to bring home enough to fill us. But at least there is almost always something to chew on.

"The plants are just a little different here," I tell Celia, gnawing on a sassafras twig. Its root beer taste helps keep the hunger at bay. All of those walks I took with my parents so many years ago must have made some impression. More and more I begin to recognize plants, develop a sense of what is edible, what is not. When I'm uncertain, I hold whatever I've found . . . a leaf, a mushroom, a berry, a root . . . against the underside of my arm, then against my lips, then on my tongue. Only after that will I take the smallest bite.

Celia has trouble keeping certain things down. I think it's my fault, though I never seem to get sick.

"Have you always had trouble with your stomach?" I ask.

Celia shrugs, her way of letting me know she doesn't like the subject. She hates admitting weakness of any sort. This I've learned quickly in our short time together.

Today we sit on the step of the schoolhouse and munch small, tart berries.

"There's this place in Brattleboro," I tell her. "A cornfield at the top of a trail. Through the winter, even in spring and early summer, before the corn gets too high, you can stand in the middle of it and see for miles and miles."

Celia squints at me, her pale eyes studying me intently. "I like the way you say things, Radley."

I shrug, offer her some sassafras to go with the berries. She accepts with a nod.

"Not far from here there's a path up into the woods," I tell her. "It's steep once you get in there. Not as bad as those last few days before we got here. But steep enough to keep your heart pounding. Sometimes the mist clings to the trees in there and I feel like I'm walking in the clouds. It's pretty amazing. Definitely worth the effort. You'd like it, I think. You should come along sometime."

Celia wraps her arms around Jerry Lee and rests her chin on the dog's furry back. "No," she says. "I don't think so."

"Did you tell anyone you were leaving," I ask Celia one night as we wait for sleep. "Any of your family, friends?"

"No one," Celia says. "Maybe a few people are wondering where I am. But not many. When I was younger my cousins and I would go to my grandmother's house a couple times a year. Most times we kids would go out on the street and leave the adults in the house to drink and fight. It was fun having all those cousins around. Then my grandmother died and everybody sort of lost touch. With you, Radley, it feels kind of like when the cousins came."

"Well, we've certainly left the *house* so the adults can fight."

"Pretty big house to walk away from, the whole United States," Celia says.

"Pretty big fight, too," I say. And I wonder for the thousandth time where my parents are.

I'm at the brook, washing dirt off and picking worms out of vegetables left for us by Our Lady of the Barn. I don't know why I bother. The worms won't hurt us.

Back at the schoolhouse I look at the *meal* we've put together on the rough table. Celia has fashioned a little centerpiece from bits of things she's found. This primitive little place of ours is such a sharp contrast to my parents' elegant home.

I think about the differences between Haiti and the

house on Channing Street, and this schoolhouse in the woods of southern Quebec. I've been a different Radley in all three places. I'm not certain which is the real Radley.

"I never knew how much people judged you by your appearance or where you lived until all this started," I say.

"You're kidding, right?" Celia says. "Even you can't be that innocent, Radley."

"I know. It's just that as far as I could tell, my parents never judged anyone. And they really rode me when *I* did it."

"Okay." Celia shrugs. "Maybe there are a few people in the world who don't judge you by what they see on the outside, but only a few."

The broccoli barely hits her stomach when Celia tears out the door. I know she's throwing it up. I save half of mine. Maybe she'll be able to hold something down a little later.

After she returns, I'm frightened by how pale she is, how frail she is.

"Celia, do you think we should turn ourselves in? Maybe you should see a doctor . . ."

"You're crazy, Radley."

"If you're hungry later . . . I couldn't finish . . ."

Celia is silent. Her temper usually flares when she thinks I've intentionally done something kind for her. I can see irritation written on her face. But rather than fight with me, she storms out and sits on the step with Jerry Lee.

Stomping away like that, it's just what I used to do to my mother all the time. I wish I could apologize to my parents right now.

By my calculations it's early July. The sun is fierce. The air drips with humidity. A mist of hungry insects swarm, pinning us inside the schoolhouse, which is oppressively hot and stuffy. Even inside we're not free of bugs. But there are certainly fewer inside than out.

Whenever the day is close like this the wild animal stench we first encountered when we opened the place returns, rising out of the wood.

We stretch out on the splintery floor and gaze at the ceiling with its stained and busted tiles. I miss my parents so much. I wonder what's going on in the States now. In our little schoolhouse at the edge of civilization we are so isolated from the rest of the world. In some ways I'm grateful for the peace of it. In some ways it fills me with despair to be so cut off.

"Do you ever want to just give up, Celia?" My voice is barely above a whisper.

"You mean turn ourselves in?"

"No," I say. "I mean really give up. You know . . . off yourself."

I turn toward her and see a shadow pass over her face.

"Do you have a boyfriend?" Celia asks.

"No. Why?"

"Just wondering."

"Do you?"

Celia gives a quick shake no and is quiet for awhile.

Finally, she turns to face me. "I could never kill myself, Rad. I like fried onions too much."

I feel something shift inside me and suddenly I'm lighter. I don't know how she does it.

"Celia, we don't have fried onions. You couldn't keep them down even if we did."

Celia smiles. It's a strange smile. "Possibly the only thing I *could* keep down."

I promise myself a trip to Sutton later, after dark. I vow to check every Dumpster and trash bin until I find what Celia's longing for.

To pass the time, I tell Celia about the cowgirl dress from my grandmother. I describe it in all its hideous detail.

"But, Celia, I swear I'd wear it every day if only I could have my old life back again."

Celia snorts. "A cowgirl dress? Really? You'd wear it every day?"

"Yup."

"Forget the police, Radley. You'd better be watching out for the fashion guards."

The two of us in our worn farm clothes and our chopped hair, stuck inside a rotting, mildewed schoolhouse, begin to laugh. Celia holds her stomach and rolls on the floor with glee. I hear a sound coming from her I've never heard before. I'm not certain Jerry Lee has heard it either. He butts her over and over again with his head.

When we finally grow still, the silence is unnerving.

"Tell me where you really were when all this started," Celia says.

And I tell her about Haiti. I tell her how I had no idea what I was getting into when I went there. How there wasn't enough food, or water. I tell her how the orphanage was an old, abandoned schoolhouse. "But nothing like this one. The kids couldn't even go outside the gate."

I fall silent, thinking about Celia not venturing more than a few feet from the schoolhouse door. I wonder if she's thinking the same.

"I wish I could build them a new orphanage in a safe neighborhood where they could grow their own food, have clean water.

"They sleep on these flimsy cots, Ceil.

"Each night I would go from child to child for their bedtime hugs. I don't know if anyone hugged them before I came. I don't know if anyone hugs them now that I've gone.

"Celia, there were so many children, there was so much need. There was this little boy, Jean-Claude. He was maybe four. He would tell me he had a stomachache when really he was just hungry. I'd rub his back to comfort him the way my mother rubbed mine when I was small.

"Jean-Claude had lived on the streets for months. No one knows what he endured before he came to the orphanage. He wouldn't talk about it. He couldn't talk about it."

Just like you, Ceil, I think. But I don't say that out loud.

I gather a handful of daisies on my way back to the school-house with the soggy onion rings I've found for Celia.

My mother loves daisies. When I was small and we were living from paycheck to paycheck, Mom made do with less food so she could buy daisies at the grocery store. It never occurred to my mother that she could go out and pick wild daisies. That she could have them for free.

She would often leave a jar of them on the nightstand beside my bed. I hated daisies. I hated the way they smelled, particularly after they started to slime.

Now *I* gather daisies. I pick a handful with their white-slip petals and their tawny eyes and place them in a bottle I've found by the side of the road. I bring them to the schoolhouse and set them on the floor by our bed.

Celia eats only a bite of the onion rings, then pushes the rest away. Moments later she's outside heaving her guts up.

"I guess I was wrong," Celia says. "About being able to hold down fried onions."

"Don't tell her," I whisper to Jerry Lee, "but I hate when she's wrong."

Celia comes over, kneels, wraps her arms around Jerry Lee's chest, lays her head gently on his back, and sighs. "I hate it, too."

Celia loves movies, particularly action and animation. I love movies, too, mostly fantasy and comedy and love stories. We alternate telling movie plots to each other.

Occasionally we hit on a movie we have in common. Or an entire series . . . like the Harry Potters.

It is then, particularly, we see how in some ways we are so alike.

Our Lady of the Barn leaves a copy of the *Montreal Gazette* for us. My French is pretty good but I'm still glad to have an English-language newspaper.

I fold it carefully and carry it home along with the fresh vegetables she's left. I handle the newspaper like a holy relic. Not only does it tell us the date (July 12) and the weather forecast, but it connects us to the outside world.

I read aloud to Celia while she stares out the window. A half-dozen letters to the editor debate the subject of civil rights under emergency law. Eyewitness reports describe overcrowded U.S. prisons and outbreaks of disease. The paper says American television transmission is mostly down, newspaper publication spotty, and access to the Internet completely unreliable; it's hard to say how rampant the looting, violence, and general criminal activity truly is. All the news from the States is anecdotal.

In the classifieds, people advertise safe houses and I ask Celia what she thinks.

"I think about that sleazebag who tried to pick us up in Vermont. I think we'd be crazy to risk it."

I wonder how many others there are, people like us trying to survive, relying on the kindness of strangers. I wonder how many have trusted the wrong people.

I pray my parents haven't trusted the wrong people.

How I wish to see her, our benefactress.

At dusk, lingering in the woods a safe distance from the barn, I wait. Finally, well after dark, I catch sight of her. By the light of the moon an ancient woman with a stooped back shuffles through the unkempt garden. I listen as she talks to the weeds, to the plants, to the clods of dirt. I watch her move from the garden to the barn, from the barn to the house. She never switches on a light.

After she disappears into her home, I enter the garden where the gate hangs on one hinge. Weeds grasp my ankles. Something sharp slices my skin. How did the old woman move through here so smoothly?

Back in the barn I find a dimpled rump of cauliflower waiting for me.

I place Our Lady's offering in my rusted bucket and scratch a note into the wood with my pocket knife. "Thanks."

Celia and I divide the head exactly in half. I tell her everything I have seen and each bite of spicy white cauliflower tastes like a miracle.

"You could pull weeds for her," Celia suggests.

I nod. "You could, too."

"No," Celia says firmly.

"No?"

"No."

Something in her tone makes the hair lift on my neck.

"Why? Why don't you ever leave this room?"

But Celia has nothing more to say.

It's midday. I've managed to get Celia back to the brook behind the schoolhouse by telling her I refuse to wash her underwear. If she wants clean knickers she'll have to scrub them herself.

How did she have the courage to travel all the way from

Windsor, when now she's afraid to go five yards from the schoolhouse?

We hand wash our clothes in a circle of sunlight. The sliver of soap from Our Lady of the Barn is nearly gone. I hope soon she remembers to leave more.

"I like it here," Celia says.

"Here? By the brook?"

"No," Celia says. "Here. This life. Canada."

I shake my head. "Celia, you never leave the schoolhouse. You can't go more than twelve hours without throwing your guts up. But you like it here?"

"Yeah. I do."

"Why?" I ask. "Why do you like it here?"

"I feel so free here."

"Free?"

"Yeah. I don't have any history here. No one judges me. And you feed me. I feel like someone's taking care of me for the first time in my life. I have no responsibilities. It feels good."

"You're responsible for Jerry Lee," I say.

"That's never felt like a job. Besides, Jerry Lee can take

care of himself." Celia smiles fondly down at the dog, who gazes back at her just as fondly. "In my whole life, he's the only one I've ever been able to count on. Until you."

I don't say anything. I just keep rinsing out my bra. I have only the one and I'm careful with it. What *can* I say anyway? You shouldn't count on me? I'm doing a crap job of taking care of you? You vomit up everything I ever bring to you?

And then, out of the blue, she says, "You know what I really miss, though?"

She doesn't wait for an answer.

"I really miss tuna sandwiches."

I burst out laughing. She can hardly keep water down, nearly everything she puts in her stomach comes back up again, and yet the thing she likes to talk about most is food, either fried or swimming in mayonnaise or butter.

My fingers fumble and my clean, wet bra lands in a patch of brown pine needles. First I try picking the needles off, but there are too many. I slap the bra back into the water to rinse again.

"I miss tuna fish sandwiches, too," I say.

My mind goes leaping to my parents' kitchen and my mother draining a can of tuna over the sink and Romulus rubbing against her leg, crazy with wanting.

"I like it with those crispy fried onions on top," Celia says. "You know the kind that come in a can? You know which ones I mean?"

I nod. Why am I not surprised?

Our situation feels less perilous with each week we're here. The Canadians don't seem to have the will to hunt us down, to send us back. I start venturing out in daylight. I'm familiar enough with the area, I know where the dogs are, where the people are. I feel safe walking these roads. When a truck putters past, the driver waves. I wave back. In a strange way I feel accepted.

It is much better out in the open. Staying inside that schoolhouse during the hottest part of the day drives me insane. I don't know how Celia bears it.

One day four ducks follow me from a pond on my way back to the schoolhouse. One comes all the way to the edge of the woods before noisily returning to its comrades.

I begin thinking about eggs. How long has it been since I've eaten an egg?

In the latest *Montreal Gazette* it says that typhoid, dysentery, cholera, tuberculosis, influenza, pneumonia, polio, and nearly every other ailment known to mankind—diseases once conquered—have broken out in the overcrowded prisons back home. People have died. It's unclear how many.

All the money we donated as a family at Christmastime over the years to CARE and Doctors Without Borders and UNICEF, we never imagined a need like this in our own country. Who could have?

It feels as if I've just fallen asleep when a fierce storm crashes down on us. Thunderstorms terrify me. When I was little I'd go rigid under the blankets on wild nights until my mother came, her feet so cold as she slid in beside me, the rest of her so warm. Romulus would follow her and the three of us would cling to each other as the storm raged outside.

Celia stands at the open door in a white shirt and bare legs, facing into the wind, into the fury. Seeing her ghostly figure outlined by spasms of lightning, I say nothing. I am filled with terror. I am filled with awe.

An occasional rumble of thunder still rolls over our roof, but mostly the storm is snapping its teeth a safe distance from here. The air around our schoolhouse has cooled. It smells sweet.

Celia slips back under the blanket. Her feet are freezing. So is the rest of her. She plucks Jethro's bear from where it teeters on the edge of the bed and holds it close.

I don't know what makes me do it. I open my arms to her the way my mother would have done. And Celia does not turn away.

"I could have stuck it out in Windsor," she says, shivering. "I didn't have any complaints with the APPs."

Celia sighs. She doesn't often sigh. "I dropped out of school when I was sixteen. Did I tell you that?"

I shake my head no.

"People think they know you. What you said the other day about people judging you, it's so true.

"In Windsor there was this guy. He ate at the diner where I worked. Always asked for me. I had a few regulars. Most of them I liked well enough. But this guy was a pain, always sending things back because they weren't right. And a lousy tipper. A real asshole.

"One night, after I locked up the restaurant, he was waiting for me outside. It was late, no one else around. He grabbed me and dragged me down the bank. I thought I was strong. I wasn't strong enough."

A long, ragged breath escapes from Celia.

"He . . ."

She swallows and tries again.

"He . . ."

But she is unable to put into words what he did to her that night. She doesn't have to.

"That's the night I left Windsor. I went back to my place only long enough to shower, put on fresh clothes, and get Jerry Lee. You found me in the woods a few days later."

Now I understood why she never left the schoolhouse. Why she locked herself inside when I was away. Even with Jerry Lee by her side to protect her.

"Are you pregnant?" I whisper.

"No. No. I can't be." And another sigh. "If I ever see him again I'll kill him."

I take her hand in the dark to warm her, to comfort her. "Don't worry," I whisper. "I'll be right beside you. You won't have to do it alone."

I wake feeling crushed by what Celia has told me. But she acts the same as always. So I follow her lead.

Out foraging, I discover a mulberry tree. Picking and eating, filling the dented pail, I am grateful to have the sun on me, to have birds winging in and out of shafts of light, and insects leaping through the tall grass. The beauty of the day helps dispel the ugliness revealed the night before.

My mother would pick mulberries from the tree behind our house every summer. She would bake the berries into pies.

I can't bake a pie. Even if we had an oven here I couldn't bake a pie. I never followed my mother into the kitchen. There was always something else I'd rather do.

When this is over, I will enter my mother's kitchen with my sleeves rolled up and I won't go away until she's taught me everything I should know about baking a pie.

And everything I should know about everything else, too.

How she'll laugh when I tell her that one day, in the midst of this ordeal, all I wanted in this sunlit moment was to be in her gleaming kitchen, wearing an apron, standing beside her, the two of us up to our wrists in flour.

At night I dream of being hunted.

Celia has nightmares, too. She thrashes in the bed and once or twice she's punched me hard enough to raise a bruise.

After three nights in a row of being woken by Celia crying out in her sleep, I say, "Enough. You have to get out of here. You're losing your mind."

And later that morning I lead Celia and Jerry Lee to the pond with the curious ducks. It's not much of a pond, mostly weeds and bracken, but the sky is cupped in its watery palm, and the sun warms us all the way to the bone.

"Breathe it in," I tell Celia.

Her skin is so pale, her mouth so grim. She's clearly uneasy being this far from the schoolhouse. But she nods and draws the fresh air into her lungs.

Side by side, we study our reflections in the water. In our dun clothes, with our wild, spiky hair we resemble two enormous nestlings blown from a tree.

Our Lady of the Barn has left two live chickens.

Chickens!

Along with a basket to carry them.

And a plastic tub with food for them to eat.

We move the bed into the front room and turn the far room into a chicken yard. Jerry Lee shows a doglike interest in chasing the chickens and they run and hide from him between my legs.

When Celia speaks sharply to him, Jerry Lee tucks in his tail and slinks guiltily back to her side.

"You're crazy, you know," Celia says, watching me clean out the back room. "It can't be healthy to live in the same house with chickens. Why don't you make a yard for them outside?"

Though I feel safe now walking along the road, encountering people from time to time, I still think it's better our home remains secret.

"If we make a yard for them outside someone might see. They've got to live inside. I'll clean up after them. What should we name them?"

Celia rolls her eyes and leaves me to my housekeeping.

I remember the barnyard photographs my mother took a couple of years ago. She won an award for them.

As I pull up splintery floorboards in the back room to reveal the dirt beneath, I talk to the chickens. "My mother would be so happy to see you guys," I murmur. "Maybe even happier to see you than to see me."

"That's not true," Celia calls, challenging me.

"What's not true?" I call back.

"About your mother."

I have to rewind to what I've just said. Ah, about my mother preferring the chickens to me.

"How do *you* know what's true about my mother?" I ask Celia. "You've never met her. Believe me, she never saw a chicken she didn't love. I, on the other hand, have not always been the model daughter."

The floorboards are beyond filthy, the dirt beneath the wooden boards totally disgusting. The chickens are constantly under foot and the work of preparing a "yard" for them in the sweltering schoolhouse has me feeling more than a little testy. All these rusty nails and beer cans; I'm grateful I got that tetanus booster before leaving for Haiti.

Celia says, "I'm willing to *bet* your mother loves you more than any *chickens*."

Now it's my turn to roll my eyes. But I think about my mother pacing in the front hall when I arrived home hours later than expected. I remember the generous amount on my dinner plate and the tiny portion on Mom's when money was tight. I remember finding her weeping silently on the sofa after we'd fought. I remember the forgiving touch of my mother when she kissed me good night, her gentle movements through the house when she nursed me through illness. I remember that whenever I asked for her attention, she stopped what she was doing and gave it to me.

Celia interrupts my thoughts. "It's the way you do things, Rad. The way you took care of me when we first met. The way you've taken care of me ever since. You knew how to do those things because your mother does them for you. That's how I know how much she loves you."

I sit watching the chickens pecking happily away in their new luxury indoor chicken yard.

I don't want to admit it but Celia's right.

"I'm thinking," I tell her, pretending to ignore what she's just said, "I'm thinking the chickens' names should be Wynonna and Ashley. Ashley's the red one."

I haven't managed to get Celia out since the day we went to the pond, but while I'm away gathering food, she starts exploring the weeds and undergrowth around the perimeter of the schoolhouse, collecting acorns, pinecones, feathery grasses, abandoned nests. She arranges the treasures

throughout our room, sometimes posing Jethro's bear in the midst of it all. It's comical to watch her chase the chickens away when they flap over to investigate. Celia's creativity astounds me. Her antics with Jerry Lee and the chickens make me laugh.

I'm so grateful that this schoolhouse has turned out to be less a prison, more a home. And it's Celia who's made it so.

I wish I could show my parents how we've managed. I hope I can remember everything when I see them again.

The day slips away and the western sky colors, and our stomachs are full enough inside our little room thanks to Our Lady of the Barn. Celia begins to hum, I to dance. I know mostly my parents' music. Celia knows the hard-edged, brittle, newer music. The music I should know. The music I would know if my parents weren't such funny old hippies.

We have a vast library of songs between us, particularly when I add in the music of the orphans.

Dancing and singing make the time pass.

The chickens like it, too.

They've started laying eggs! Eggs! The chickens are laying eggs!

There are two of them waiting for us this morning.
Warm, beautiful, perfect eggs.

"We're eating raw eggs?" Celia asks.

I've been fantasizing about eggs for weeks. "We've got to cook them," I say.

"Radley, how do you plan to do that?"

Back in sixth-grade science class we made solar cookers with boxes and black paint. I might find a couple of boxes when I'm out exploring, but where am I going to find black paint?

"We'll need a fire," I admit, thinking of the matches I brought from home.

"But a fire would draw attention to us," Celia says.

I nod. "Okay, here's what I'm thinking. We dig a little hole, we line it with rocks. Put some dried grass in it, then some twigs."

Celia is listening but her face has that this-is-never-going-to-work look.

"It will work, Celia. We've got a couple of tin cans. We let some water sit in them, warming up in the sun while we get a little fire going, a little one, and we put the eggs in

173

the warm water in the cans, put the cans in the fire on top of the stones, and feed just enough twigs and grass into the flames to get the water to boil. We can do this."

Celia's smile is lopsided with doubt.

But I'm certain we can do it.

And we do.

With hardly any smoke.

I go off for some distance and check to see how visible our little cooking experiment is.

In the end, although the eggs aren't exactly hard-boiled, they're not raw either.

Now I love Wynonna and Ashley not only because they entertain us, but because they feed us, too. Can there be anything more wonderful than a chicken? Finally I get why my mother is so crazy about them.

My egg, when I finally bite into it, tastes more delicious than any meal I can ever remember.

And now we know that we can cook. At least a little. And we can make hot water, and hot rocks. "Next goal . . . coffee," I say, egg yolk clinging to my teeth.

"Proud of yourself, aren't you, Rad," Celia says as she catches some egg bits with her finger and tucks them back into her mouth.

I nod, noticing with joy that Celia is having no trouble keeping this meal down.

"You *should* be proud of yourself," Celia says. "Now, if you could just make salt?"

On Celia's birthday, what we think is Celia's birthday, I steal a small melon. I pick a handful of wildflowers.

I remember the restaurants where we, as a family, went on birthdays over the years. I remember the cake my mother baked in the shape of a teddy bear when I was six; I remember the trays of cupcakes with glitter and thick chocolate icing I'd take to school to share with my class-mates.

I remember the gifts: the books, the games, the spinning wheel. The spinning wheel had been bought by my parents from a man grieving the death of his wife. They were so pleased to give it to me. I had learned to spin at school and "showed a talent for it," my teacher said.

But I could never bring myself to sit at that wheel. It had the man's grief in it. It had the wife's ghost sitting there where they expected me to sit. How could I spin wool on it? Who could wear anything knit from wool spun on that wheel?

My parents kept it anyway, even though I never touched it. One day, while I was at school, they moved it out of my room, down to the basement. Never said a word about it. Just one day it was blessedly out of my sight.

I vow that I will spin on that wheel when I get home. I'll make yarn for my mother to knit. And I will love everything she makes for me. Everything.

Celia is remembering past birthdays too, I think.

Neither of us says much.

But we gnaw on the melon right down to the rind. What remains goes to Ashley and Wynonna, who are elated.

Our Lady of the Barn leaves a small loaf of bread for us. To taste fresh homemade bread, no butter, no jam, simply the wheat of it, the yeast of it, the salt of it, fills me with happiness. To see Celia enjoy food again and keep it down is such a relief.

I have no reason to feel so but I am utterly content. It's strange. I let the feeling work its way through me, I fix the sensation of it under my skin so that I can call it up again when I need it.

For this moment I don't think about the political and social mayhem south of here, about the gangs, the murders, the sickness spreading to every corner of the U.S. I don't think about my parents and what has befallen them. In an hour I'll think of those things, or tomorrow.

But right now, I am content.

The light this morning strokes the splintery wooden floor of our schoolhouse. Out the door, the dissolving mist transforms our little clearing into a fairyland of sparkling dew.

I ignore the demands of the chickens, button into my ink-stained shirt, my pants, my boots, and walk into the gleaming morning.

For the first time, Jerry Lee leaves Celia and comes with me.

One of the articles in a recent newspaper left by Our Lady of the Barn says that every eligible American between the ages of eighteen and thirty who is not already a member of the military, must, starting immediately, give two years of public service. The "volunteers" are not even consulted about type of work or location. They are being sent anywhere in the country the government needs them. And from the sound of it, the government needs them everywhere.

The president calls this "an opportunity to be on the ground floor of restoring the country's balance." Congress is calling it "a redistribution of talent." They're touting "the glory of serving one's country in its time of great need."

But if you ask me, I'd say they've got a lot of nerve. They broke the country. They should be out there fixing it themselves.

The night is hot. We sleep in our T-shirts on top of the blanket.

Nocturnal animals rustle outside the flimsy walls. I hear them in the dried leaves.

The chickens murmur softly in their sleep.

I am wide-awake, staring at the ceiling. Celia, it seems, is also sleepless.

We talk more at night, side by side in the dark, than we do during the hours of daylight. The topics of our night talks

are often forbidden subjects during the day. Something about the intimacy of the dark makes us more open with each other.

"Do you think, Radley, that we come back after we die?" Celia asks quietly.

"You mean like ghosts?"

"No," Celia says. "Like in a new body."

"Reincarnation?" I ask.

"Yeah," Celia says. "That."

"I don't know," I answer. "Maybe."

"Who would you want to be the next time you come back?" Celia asks.

"What will the world be like then? Like it was before the APPs? Like the world we're in now? Or like the world at the end of all this?"

Celia is quiet for a moment. "Like the world will be after this is over and forgotten."

"This will never be forgotten, Ceil. Unless you're thinking millions of years from now . . . when humans are extinct."

Celia sighs, exasperated.

"Who do *you* want to be the next time?" I ask her.

"I want to be the daughter of a famous photographer," she says softly.

For the first time since we've been together I intentionally turn my back on Celia.

Pressing my palms hard against my eyes, I wait for the wave of longing to subside.

I crave a hot shower, a flush toilet, light switches, a washing machine. I want a chair and a sofa and a mattress. I yearn for clothes that fit, shampoo that lathers . . . I ache for scented things, girly things. I want a pantry full of food and a stove to cook it on.

I will not take anything for granted should this ever end, should I find my way back to civilization. I will be such a good daughter. My parents won't even know me.

I always stop at Our Lady of the Barn first to see if there's anything waiting for me. Then I head into Sutton. It's hours of walking each day, but though I am always hungry, I am also more fit than I've ever been in my life.

In Sutton, the owner of the restaurant who caught me so soon after we arrived often stops me now with wrapped-up parcels of food to take back to the schoolhouse.

Carrying her generous care packages, I remember, in

Haiti, tearing open bricks of instant noodles sent by my parents. I would hold a child on my hip while the water boiled. Another would lean against my leg. The cook, Eulalie, always managed to turn the brittle twigs into such tasty meals.

And later, before bed, with our stomachs well pleased, the children would sing with me, or they would clamor for stories, just as Celia does, stories of snow, stories of my big house, and my clever cat.

How I miss the purring of Romulus in my lap. There were cats in Haiti but they were wild. The children purred in my lap instead. And here? Here the chickens do the same.

And it is almost as good.

I'm unpacking the pail filled with the most recent offerings from Our Lady of the Barn. Normally Celia pulls the objects out, one at a time, spreading them across our rough table. But today she sits on the bed and watches.

"You okay, Celia?"

She nods.

Three tomatoes emerge from the pail and catch the sunlight. Celia usually eats fresh tomatoes straightaway, the juice rolling down her arm.

"You sure you're okay?" I ask.

She nods.

I walk two steps to the bed, place a tomato in Celia's hands, then kiss her cheeks, one at a time.

Her lashes are wet against my face.

"What is it?" I ask.

"I'm just feeling really alone."

"You're not alone," I tell her.

"When this is over you'll leave. You'll *fly* back to your parents. I'll be more alone than I've ever been in my life. It'll be just me and Jerry Lee again."

"So come home with me."

"I'd never fit in your world."

We're silent, thinking about that, about how different we are. Would it really be any harder in Brattleboro than it is here?

I wonder.

"Look," Celia says. "If it doesn't work out for you when you get home, Radley, will you promise to find me?"

I can't even find my parents and once I do I'm never letting them out of my sight. But I don't want to upset Celia.

And so I nod. "Of course I'll come find you. If things don't work out. I promise. Even if they do work out, we'll stay in touch, Celia. I can visit you. You'll come and stay with me. Honestly, your biggest problem will be how to get rid of me."

Celia smiles.

We go outside then and eat the tomatoes greedily, noisily. They taste like candy. We chew the delicate meat, our eyes half closed with pleasure.

My parents have always grown tomatoes. I remember being so little and carrying them in from the garden; how proud I was to help. I remember the sun's warmth lingering inside the firm red globes.

Nothing ever tasted as good as those tomatoes warm from my parents' garden.

These come a close second though.

I'm thinking I might catch some fish," I tell Celia, examining the pole and hooks left this morning by Our Lady of the Barn. "Want to come?"

"Nope."

I stand there, unwilling to drop the matter. "Won't you please come?"

"Nope," Celia says again.

"I need you to come, Celia. I don't know how to do it."

Celia gives me a scathing look. "You put a worm on the hook, you put the hook in the water. It's pretty easy."

"But I don't know what to do with the fish once it's caught. I don't know how to clean it or anything."

Celia says, "If you catch a fish, bring it to me. I'll take care of it."

So I become a fisherman.

I sit for hours between bites. I like that. I went fishing with my grandfather when I was little. He didn't keep anything he caught. He told me he just liked being outside.

When a fish took his bait, he'd reel it in, gently unhook it, talking calmly to it the whole time, and then, as carefully as possible, he'd place it back in the water. I hated that he died before I really got to know him. But I'm glad he didn't live to see the country turn on itself like it has.

I don't release my catch the way my grandfather did, but I do talk to it.

When I get the fish back to the schoolhouse, Celia guts it and cooks it over our small fire.

I thought boiled eggs tasted pretty great but fresh fish is even better.

Celia licks her fingers, one at a time.

I give myself permission to build a slightly larger fire the next time and we char the fish I've caught.

Blowing gently on the twigs, I watch their tips light up like cigarette ends.

"Do you know the story of your birth?" Celia asks.

I am surprised by the question. It's more a middle-of-the-night question than a dinner question, but I nod.

"Tell me," Celia says.

"There was a snowstorm," I say. "The midwife's car went off the road on her way to our house. A stranger picked her up, gave her a lift, and watched my mother give birth to me." Celia shakes her head in wonder.

"The most amazing part of the story is that after the midwife left, my mother, with me in her arms, rose from her bed and looked out the window over the fresh snow. The way she tells it, the storm had passed and the sky was the color of sapphires. As my mother watched, a hawk dropped from that immense blueness and caught an unsuspecting jay in midair. The windows, closed against the cold, couldn't possibly have let the sound in and yet my mother heard the death scream of the blue jay. On the day I was born."

Celia shudders.

"And you?" I ask. "Do you know the story of your birth?"

"My mother, when her labor started, told my father that she needed to go to the hospital. He didn't believe her so she drove herself. She gave birth to me outside the emergency room. The nurses on duty that day still tease me about it."

Celia is silent for a moment. "It's the best story I've got, Radley, and yours is still better."

"This isn't a competition, Celia."

"I know," Celia says.

A piece of fish drops onto the stone in our fire pit. "It's yours," I say.

Celia deftly plucks up the delicate flesh with her fingers and eats it without letting it cool.

"Ow."

"Burn your tongue?" I ask.

Celia nods. "Why are you smiling?"

"Remember when you didn't think we could make a fire hot enough to boil an egg?"

Daylight enters at a new angle on the schoolhouse floor. A few leaves change color. It grows cooler at night.

Though winter is still many months away, I worry how we can possibly last here in this unheated, ramshackle schoolhouse.

In the afternoon I wander into an overgrown orchard. Apples, small and hard, adorn the boughs.

I lie down under the trees on a mattress of grass, remembering picking apples last fall with my parents, and drift into a blissful sleep.

When I wake the sun is low in the sky.

Celia sits on the schoolhouse step, waiting. It is fully dark by the time I catch sight of her. The sky winks with stars.

"I was worried," she says.

"I'm sorry," I answer.

"Where were you?"

"I fell asleep in an apple orchard."

Celia rises, rubbing her back, stiff from sitting so long. She huffs inside the schoolhouse.

She's angry.

But I'm not certain if she's angrier at me or at herself.

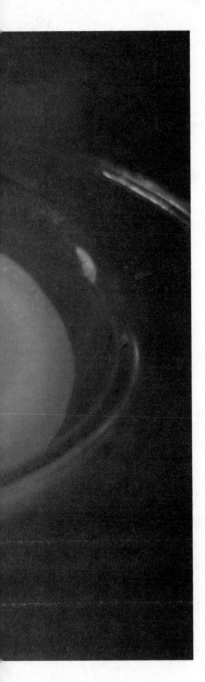

We receive a box of matches and a single candle from our benefactress. My matches were running low. I'm relieved to see these.

We don't dare light the candle at night. If we light it at all it's only for a few moments, before daylight is entirely gone, before the candlelight would be visible from our windows.

We light the candle because it brings us peace, even as it uses up a precious match. We lean into the light, cup its warmth in our palms, then blow it out before the sky grows any darker.

When hunting season begins we won't dare light it at all.

At night we pick a room in our old homes and describe it. My house is large, larger than any place Celia has ever lived. I have more rooms to describe. But Celia has lived in more places, and she remembers more in each room. This, too, she teaches me.

I tell her about the spinning wheel and my plan to start using it when I get back home.

"You really think it'll still be there?" she asks.

"Why shouldn't it be? I locked the house when I left."

"Yeah, it's all probably fine," Celia says.

"You think someone's going to break in and steal a spinning wheel? Really? Who would do that?"

"No one, I guess. But who knows. Maybe you won't even want that stuff when you get home."

I start to argue with her, but then, when I think about it, when I think of how little we actually need here at the schoolhouse, when I think about how the children at Paradis des Enfants manage with so little, I realize Celia's probably right.

"Celia, you're so smart," I say.

It's too dark to see her but I hear her. I hear the sound of her smile.

We're eating our way through a bucket of wild blueberries and I'm thinking about the children's librarian in Brattleboro and the summer I volunteered up on the second floor, shelving books, helping with story time, filing.

I tell Celia about the librarian . . . how she was in charge of the entire floor.

"I remember she loved books about dogs. And wombats. And pigs. But what I most remember about her is that she baked chocolate brownies for the staff every now and then. They were the kind of brownies where the chocolate sticks to your teeth. You know that kind?"

Celia nods.

"They were so good, Celia. Better than any brownies I ever tasted. I mean it. Those brownies made me so happy. I'd give my life if I could have a plate of those brownies right now."

Celia's tongue is stained purple. She scrapes blueberry goo out from under her fingernails. "Your life? Really? You wouldn't give your life, Radley."

"Yes," I say. "Yes. I would."

Celia looks long at me. "And never see your parents again?"

"My mother would understand. It's a chocolate thing."

Celia snorts.

But I'm still thinking about that librarian. I wonder how she's doing through all of this.

How did you ever manage to talk your parents into letting you go to Haiti?"

The days have grown hot again and tonight the insects sing outside the schoolhouse. Celia and I sweat on top of our blankets.

"Well, when I first proposed spending time in an impoverished, earthquake-devastated country, I expected my parents to shoot the idea down. I never thought they'd say yes.

"But Mom said, '*Of course you should go.*'

"My dad wasn't crazy about the idea. He was more concerned that I finish the school year.

"But my mom said, '*She'll learn more in Haiti than she'll learn here.*'

"Dad argued that there were already too many half-educated people in the world. That our family didn't need to contribute to the problem."

I tell Celia Dad thinks that's the way the APPs got so far in such a short time.

"He says a poorly educated populace makes bad choices in the voting booth. Dad says the earthquake in Haiti wouldn't have been nearly so bad if all the houses had been built right. But the houses weren't built right because there was no standard. And there was no standard because the people were undereducated. Dad says that's where we're heading in the U.S., too."

Celia says, "Is that what it's like in your house all the time? Do you guys, like, always go on and on like that?"

"Pretty much," I say.

"No wonder you wanted to get out of town," Celia says.

"Yeah, I guess."

"So, what happened? About going to Haiti, I mean."

I turn to Celia. "Do you really want to hear all this?"

Celia nods. I can see her wild-haired silhouette in the starlight.

"Okay. Well, in the end my mom convinced my dad and I didn't have to do a thing. They found the orphanage, bought my ticket, made things right at school. They shipped everything I needed ahead so I wouldn't have to carry too much. I just threw a few things in my backpack . . ."

"The same backpack you're using now?" Celia asks.

"Yup. Same one. Anyway, the last night I spent with my parents, we were in the kitchen making dinner together. My father said, *'It's good you're getting out while you can, Rad. Maybe you should stay in Haiti.'*"

"It was always like that. If Mom was *for* something, Dad was against it. Then Dad would be persuaded that Mom was right. But the next thing you knew, Mom had changed *her* mind."

Celia laughs.

"There were times they drove me crazy . . ."

"I can see why."

"Mom made butter beans that last night. You like butter beans, Ceil?"

"I'm not sure I've ever eaten them," she answers, but her response comes out slowly, as if she's getting sleepy.

"They're good. Big, fat white beans. I'll make butter bean salad someday for you when you come to visit. Anyway, that night at the table I told my parents I thought the APPs were a bunch of idiots.

"'*No,*' my father said. '*Don't underestimate them, Radley.*' Dad said maybe the APPs didn't know history, maybe they didn't know the Constitution. But they knew how to twist the truth. He just hoped whatever they did during their administration wasn't irreversible."

Celia sighs beside me. "Some things aren't reversible." Her voice has that slurry sound to it and I know she's drifting off.

"Good night, Ceil," I say.

"Night," she answers softly.

Celia sleeps, but my mind won't shut down. It startled me that night to hear my dad admit the government could do something that couldn't be undone, that couldn't be fixed.

Nothing surprises me anymore.

I listen to Celia, safe for the moment, rocking in the dark hammock of sleep. I'm glad for her, but the steady puff of her breath makes me feel even lonelier.

I bathe in the brook, using my ribbed undershirt as a wash-cloth, scrubbing my shirt and myself at the same time.

I get Celia to come down and bathe, too. But she's gotten surprisingly modest in the last few weeks. Maybe because

I'm always ragging her about how thin she is. With her back to me, I can see each knobby bone of her spine. But I bite my tongue and say nothing.

After our baths we look better, smell better, feel better.

"You sure you don't have a boyfriend?" Celia asks as we warm up, sitting on the schoolhouse step in the sun.

I shake my head no. I've already told her I don't.

"Who's the boy in the photograph, then?"

I fetch my mother's pictures and sort through them. It's mostly food and scenery and chickens. Not too many people.

"This guy?"

Celia nods.

I have to think a moment to remember who he is. "It's a portrait of a boy from Burundi. He lived across the street from us. That whole house was filled with international students. I wonder what all of this has done to them."

I study along with Celia my mother's portrait of the boy. I remember his name. Julian. Julian in his neatly pressed blue shirt, his head cocked slightly at the camera.

I remember the afternoon last summer when he and I sat on my porch steps and talked.

"He's very beautiful," I tell Celia. "And very brave. I think he witnessed horrible things in Burundi. But he never talked about it. I can't imagine what the last few months have been like for him."

Celia holds the picture in her hand.

"You like him?" I ask.

She shrugs. "He's not bad."

"Um-hmm," I say.

Celia rolls her eyes, hands back the photograph, and heads inside the schoolhouse. But not before I see the smile play across her lips.

I must be going out of my mind, because they are dirty and stupid and they smell nasty, but I can sit and watch Ashley and Wynonna for hours.

Celia won't admit it, but she likes watching them, too.

I'll come home from my forays to find Jerry Lee, his paws crossed, his chin resting on his elegant legs, his eyes shifting alertly from one chicken to the other. When I point him out to Celia, she grins and nods.

The feathery shuffling of the chickens lulls us to sleep at night and wakes us in the morning.

Of all the gifts from Our Lady of the Barn it is the chickens for which I am most grateful.

We wake in the morning to rain slamming against the
roof. We've had rain before but never this hard.

"Let's shift things around to keep what we've got dry," I
tell Celia.

After we've rearranged the schoolhouse, we climb into
our bed of fresh grass and cattails and pull up our blanket.
Celia lays her head beside my shoulder. We nap like that
most of the day with the drumming rain singing a lullaby
to us in its watery voice. I dream of my mother. She is sitting on the side of the bed. She smells of wildflowers and
sunlight.

In the late afternoon the storm clears. We sit on the

schoolhouse step. The woods around us shimmer with green and mist and raindrops.

"How long were you in Haiti?" Celia asks.

"I left Brattleboro shortly before the inauguration. And came back to the States right after the assassination. It was so strange being in Haiti through all of that. We didn't have a radio. There was a television but we never had power for more than an hour a day. Mostly, news came off the street. It wasn't reliable."

"It wasn't reliable in the U.S., either," Celia says.

"What did you think of her?" I ask

"Who?"

"The president," I say.

Celia shrugs. "The president? I didn't really care."

"My parents hated her, *and* her party. Remember how I said my parents weren't judgmental? Well, they were when it came to the APPs."

Celia says, "I didn't pay attention to any of it. I'm not even signed up to vote."

"I wish I'd been *old* enough to vote."

"Would it have made a difference?" Celia asks.

I sigh. "Probably not. But I still wish I had the choice. You should register for the next election, Celia. If there ever is a next election."

Celia throws off the blanket. "Maybe I will. But right now I'm hungry. Do we have anything to eat in this house?"

"No," I say.

Celia sighs. "I knew that."

Celia and I play a game. One of us picks a date—month, day, year—and the other must tell the story of that day.

"January 7, 2009," I say.

Celia invents the clothes she wore that day, the food she ate, the things she did, the people she saw, the conversations she had.

It's like writing a story. We gather the crumbs of memories, then stretch the truth until it's no longer recognizable.

Celia is far better at this game than I am.

I hear geese honking over-head. Surely it's too early for geese to be migrating south.

Stepping down into the chicken room, I rest my filthy face in my filthy hands. I feel the bone of my spine against the dirt floor.

The sound of the geese overhead, reaching me through the shoddy roof, fills me with despair. In autumn that honking always meant Thanksgiving, the house filling with aromas that dragged me to the kitchen; the sound of geese meant family, the sound of geese meant home.

Home.

Celia finds me sitting on the dirt floor with the chickens. Ashley has flapped into my lap and I stroke her as if she were a cat.

"Radley," Celia says, "you think too much. Soon this will be over. It'll be just a weird memory for you. Nothing more. Your life'll go back to normal in no time. Quit feeling sorry for yourself. If you want to feel sorry for someone, you should feel sorry for the APPs."

I stare at her, dumbfounded. "Why should I feel sorry for them?"

"Because, Radley, they have to live with what they did for the rest of their lives," Celia says.

I wonder if she's really thinking about the APPs or if she's thinking about the man from the diner. Or maybe the creep in the car. Or the thugs who pushed down the barn. I remember the waitress in the pizza place, and the woman who threw her sandwich at me from her car, and the night of the fists. I'm quiet for a while.

Finally I ask, "Ceil, would you turn back time if you could? Do things differently?"

"You're crazy, Rad. Nobody can do that. Anyway, I don't like to look back."

"The future isn't going to be all that pretty either."

"I suppose not. But, Radley, I definitely don't want to live *my* life over again. You understand that, don't you?"

I nod. Of course I do.

But that doesn't keep me from wanting to live my life over.

"When we took family vacations," I tell Celia, "we never went to the same place twice. We were always looking for something new, something we'd never done before."

"Well, your parents should be enjoying the heck out of all this then," Celia says.

I throw a handful of grass at her. Ashley and Wynonna cackle and chase the floating green blades in a chicken-and-grass ballet. Jerry Lee, who usually resists barking, emits a muffled chortle of doggie glee.

And the tension is broken.

I look skyward at yet another flock of migrating birds.

"The geese," I murmur.

Celia sits beside me on the schoolhouse step.

"I'm certain it's too early for them to be on the move but three days in a row now . . ."

"Maybe they know something," Celia says. "Maybe it's a sign . . ."

In my constant search for food, in my ever-widening circle of exploration, I come upon a pond ringed by willows.

I sit on the bank and decide that even though it's a long walk from the schoolhouse, I will bring Celia here. There is something about this place. The pond, the trees, the

reflection of leaf and sky; the green air is as good a gift as any I could make her.

For an entire afternoon I sit beside the water and forget my melancholy, my fears. My heart has a lightness to it as I imagine different ways in which the world might still come out right in the end.

On my way back to the schoolhouse I gather sweet grass and seed heads and berries, all things the chickens like to eat.

I bring them for Wynonna and Ashley. I bring them for Celia, too.

Celia and I walk into the dawn, into the sleepy arms, into the pink fields of sunrise. I know the patterns of this place. I know when it is safe to be out, where it is safe to be out.

Celia comes with surprisingly little resistance and after a mile or so, after she's come fully awake, we begin to talk easily, walking side by side.

When I was young, I loved talking with my mother while she drove the car. Conversations in profile. I loved the freckles across her cheek, and her lashes, so long even

without mascara. I learned more about my mother on those drives, she about me, than we ever managed across the dining room table.

When at last Celia sees the pond, she stops and puts her hands on her hips. Her eyes widen and she is completely silent.

"It's for you, Ceil," I say.

"I love it here," she says.

I nod. I'd hoped she would. There are so many beautiful places I want to show her. And now, at last, I think she's ready.

The next afternoon I draw Celia out again and this time we ease our bodies down between corn rows in a field about a half hour's walk from the schoolhouse. The sound of geese surrounds us. Knots of geese feed and gossip as they gather amid the towering stalks. We are almost asleep when a large dog on the far side of the field begins barking. Jerry Lee is instantly on his feet. With a single gesture,

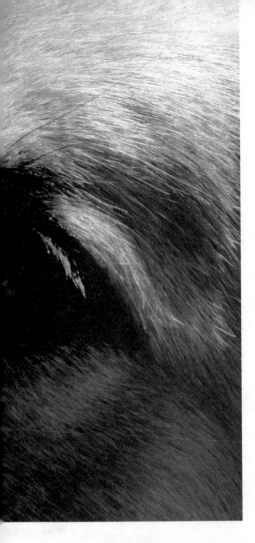

Celia commands him to get back down, to be silent. And he obeys.

In a wild frenzy the geese lift at once from the ground, their wings beating hard to escape the hold of gravity. They honk furiously.

We lie very still. The strange dog does not catch our scent. Or maybe it's not interested. We listen as it romps in the direction of the disgruntled geese who flee at a low altitude, furious at being disturbed.

In the distance we hear the come-here whistle of a human. Jerry Lee trembles as the invading dog responds to the sound, bounds off. The barking fades after a minute more.

High above, geese circle, circle, then slowly return, one group after another, settling back to their meal, grizzling all the while about the rudeness of uninvited company.

I wonder what they think of the three of us.

Another newspaper from Our Lady of the Barn. This one is full of stories about the overcrowded prisons.

The Canadian journalists report that from the beginning the insiders in the American People's Party expected to

arrest a handful of people. Certain popular bloggers. Certain well-known political agitators.

The APPs simply wanted dissenters out of the way while they "righted the wobbling ship of state." But once they started messing around with the Internet and with phone lines, such a hue and cry arose that they had to jail far more people than they ever imagined.

According to the paper, there have been numerous resignations, the arrests have stopped. And prisoners are starting to be released.

I've convinced myself that this is the fate that has befallen my parents, that they were probably some of the first to be arrested, that they'll be sent home soon.

Maybe it's time for me to head home, too.

But the high-voltage wire that rarely stops humming in my brain says, *Not yet. Not yet.*

The day dawns so softly. The air is as gentle as a fawn's breath. A brilliant blue sky wears a veil of thin clouds and the trees flounce in their new autumn colors.

I want nothing more than for this moment to last forever. How strange.

The APPs have entirely lost their grip. Even in our hiding place we sense the shift.

"I think it's over," I tell Celia.

"How do we find out for certain?"

"I'll ask someone."

"Can you risk it?"

I nod. "I can."

Celia is dead set against my going to Sutton so I use my pocket knife to scratch the question *"Over?"* in the barn directly above the place where Our Lady leaves her gifts for us.

When I return there is a package with a dress, a train schedule, and money for a single ticket. And there is a bouquet of wild flowers in a glass jar.

Written beneath my single question is a single answer.

"Yes."

It is now, only now, with the gift of the single dress, the single fare, that I realize Our Lady has no idea there are two of us. If she had known, would she have left more? I think, yes, she would have.

"The ticket should be yours," Celia says.

"I'll buy a second one for you. It's possible to use my charge card now, I think. No one will put me in prison this late in the game. Not when they're letting everyone else out."

"I don't need a ticket, Rad," Celia says. "I'm not going back."

"I can't stay here with you, Celia. You know that. I have to go home."

"I know," Celia says.

"You can't stay here alone. Not in an uninsulated, abandoned schoolhouse. Not through a Canadian winter."

"No," Celia says. "I know that. I'm not certain what I'll do. I just know I don't want to go back."

I try to persuade Celia to change her mind.

"Rad," Celia says carefully. "We both know I'm going to have a baby. I want it to be born here. In Canada."

I take a deep breath, let it slowly out, step forward, and take Celia in my arms, feel the tiniest bulge against the concavity of my own body. "How long have you been certain?"

"I think from the beginning," Celia says.

At some level I think I've known from the beginning, too.

"But how can I leave you?"

"I'll be okay. I'd always taken care of myself until you came along. I can do it again."

"It'll be different once you have a baby."

"I'll figure it out, Rad. Go home to your parents. It's all you've ever wanted to do. Go. I'll be fine."

———

The last thing I do before walking away from the school-house is to gather Wynonna and Ashley into my arms, one at a time. With Jerry Lee trotting beside us, we make our way to Our Lady's farm. It is the first time Celia has come. It is the last time I will go.

Knocking gently at the farmhouse door, I wait for our protector to answer, so I can thank her, so I can know her, so I can fix her forever in my memory, but just as it has always been, she doesn't show herself.

"Maybe she's not home," Celia says.

"Maybe."

Celia's plan is to wait in the barn until our benefactress appears, explain about the baby, and ask for her advice.

In Our Lady's barn I spread a little grain for Wynonna and Ashley. The sound of their scratching makes me smile.

Cradling Celia's face in my hands, I kiss her once on each cheek and then on her forehead. It was what my mother always did before she sent me off on a trip. Scrappy Celia allows me this demonstration of affection.

"Be safe," I tell her. "Be well."

She nods.

Sunlight catches in her lashes.

"Come back if it doesn't work out with your parents," Celia says.

"I will."

As we embrace, I inhale the scent of Celia.

Words are left unspoken. It is not the silence we knew in the beginning of our time together. That was the silence of weariness, the silence of wariness.

This silence now is the silence of grief. *This* is what Monseiur Bellamy tried to spare the children at the orphanage when he begged me not to go.

At last I understand.

I've taken Jethro's bear with me, zipped back into his old familiar pocket, because, in the end, the bear belongs to Jethro, only Jethro, and I must see to it that my tattered little companion returns to his rightful owner.

But I've left my mother's photographs back at the school-house for Celia. I won't need them anymore. Soon I'll be home.

———

I watch from the train window as scores of people make their way south on foot. Celia and I, it seems, were part of a flood of Americans who sought safety over the Canadian border.

The train crosses into Vermont in no time. I study the faces of men, women, children travelling in large groups, and sometimes there will be a profile, a tilt of head that looks familiar. But I do not see my parents.

I'll find them at the house. This time they *will* be waiting for me.

part three

The railroad tracks pass through a wonderland where rain, and sun, and cooling nights have made the countryside a tapestry of color.

It is so beautiful. It is so bountiful. It is so unreal.

———

We are instructed by the conductor to report to our town clerks the moment we arrive home so we can be included in some "record of returnees."

Who do they think will comply with such an order?

After all we've gone through, who do they think would willingly put their name on any list?

———

For months Celia has been beside me.

Now I am taunted by an empty seat. The train contains strangers. No one with whom I've shared a bed, no one I've starved with, and shivered with, laughed with, and cried with.

One man across the aisle turns his shoulder, rotating his entire body so I can't see him eating. There is something so pathetic about the angle of his torso. Something so rodentlike about the way he holds and chews his food. I wonder if he has always eaten this way. Or if this twisted consumption is a result of hiding from the APPs.

I do not eat at all. I have no hunger.

I try to ignore the perspiration under my arms, between my breasts. A heated train. I'd forgotten what artificial heat felt like . . .

I try to see the quiet beauty of Vermont, the landscape denied me these many months. I try to reclaim it as my birthright. But I know now there is no such thing as a birthright. Anything can be taken from you.

It is just missing Celia that makes me so grim, I think. But soon I'll see my parents. Then I can begin to breathe again, to live again.

In Brattleboro the familiar backside of Main Street greets the train.

I climb down the steps, hike my limp backpack up onto my shoulders, and start walking toward home. I don't even try calling in advance. I want to surprise them. To show them how I've changed.

The traffic grumbles noisily up and down the hill. Many of the storefronts stare blankly out on a late, gray afternoon. I am surprised at the number of businesses that have closed down in the four months I've been gone. But I'm also surprised at how many are still open.

I cannot walk fast enough. I'd forgotten so many of the sights along the way, but they rise before me like old friends: the mountains, the steeples, the flaming maples.

And then, there it is, standing before me. Home.

The autumn garden swirls before my eyes.

Home.

Just to see it again.

Home.

But the scene that greets me as I climb onto the porch squeezes the hope right out of my chest. Windows shattered. The front door hanging from a hinge.

My father cannot possibly be back yet. He would have fixed the door right away.

Inside, much of the furniture is gone. What remains is soiled, broken. The art has vanished from the walls. The shelves are empty. When I came back from Haiti everything had remained intact. Now I hardly recognize the house. The irony is that the house was unlocked when I arrived from Haiti. Anyone could have walked in and taken what they wanted. But no one had. When I left for Canada I locked the door behind me. Maybe I should have left it the way I found it.

I climb up the stairs to my parents' bedroom. The painting of the woman at her breakfast that hung over the fireplace is gone. My own room is destroyed. The bed and furniture, the clothes and books, my posters and prints, they're all gone. Only a rumpled blanket remains, squat in the middle of the floor.

Up in the attic my mother's desk has disappeared, too, her filing cabinets, gone. Everything, vanished.

I open the secret door in the wall, holding my breath, wondering if anything remains from the pile of things I squirreled away for safekeeping.

And it's all there, exactly as I left it when I fled to Canada in May. At least this much is preserved.

When I see the things I secreted there, waiting innocently under a thin film of dust, I grow furious at myself for not hiding more.

Why is no one here waiting for me?
The house is as empty as a lost soul.

After hours spent exploring the upper floors, I find the spinning wheel in pieces in a corner of the basement. It's so shattered that at first I don't know what I'm looking at; only a tangle of parts remain. But surely Dad can fix it. He can fix anything.

Where is my dad? I notice, for the first time, in the back of the yard, his garden tools and gloves. Everything is covered with rust and mildew. Dad never left his tools out, no matter how much of a hurry he was in.

Bringing the basket of tools back inside, a shiver runs the length of my spine. I place the rotting basket into the basement beside the remnants of the spinning wheel.

In an effort to make myself feel at home in a town that now seems so alien, I head toward the marina. I take my time, soaking it all in. This was always one of my favorite walks. My mother loved it, too, and often photographed it.

The restaurant is gone, burned to the ground. The boats that once bobbed and dipped and nodded at their moorings have also disappeared. Even the pier floating on its hollow casks has vanished.

But the giant chair remains.

I remember a father with his son and his daughter. My mother photographed them. The girl's fair hair capturing sunlight. An aura of gold floating around the child, like a saint's halo. Pressing against the back of the seat, the girl looked directly into my mother's camera, defiant. Her little brother's short blond curls danced in the breeze. He held a toy car in one hand. He never saw my mother taking his photograph. He saw only his father, who reached out to the boy, caught him, and lifted him down from the high seat. My mother captured the bliss on the boy's face. She also caught the complex expression of the daughter as her father helped *her* down. A self-conscious child resenting my mother's lens, demanding her father's total attention.

Where are those children now, I wonder. And where is their father? Was he able to lift them safely out of the horror of these last months?

I don't know why I suddenly remember something I forgot in all the stories I told Celia. My lunch bags. Every day of elementary school my father drew a picture on a brown paper lunch bag for me.

Often it would be a funny face with a clever turn of phrase pouring from its mouth into a speech bubble. All around the lunch table my friends wanted to see what my father had drawn that day.

I never thanked him. In fact I pretended to be embarrassed by him.

My father drew those faces only to delight me.

And I never thanked him.

Hunger drives me out each evening and I realize not much has changed. I am still in a holding pattern, still waiting for my parents to come home.

I can't use my credit card. The account has been frozen by the bank.

The Dumpster at the Putney Road Market provides food enough, just as it did before I left for Canada, though the owners are different now, and so is the menu.

I eat what the Dumpster offers.

I know I should look for a job.

After my parents get back . . . then I'll start looking.

I was healthier when I lived in the schoolhouse with Celia. Better fed because of Our Lady of the Barn. Because of the gardens that surrendered a potato here, a tomato there. Because of the kindness of the people of Sutton. Because of Ashley and Wynonna and their wonderful eggs. Because of the fresh fish cooked on hot rocks.

No one looks after me now and there is no one for me to look after. I wonder how Celia is doing.

———

Every day more people straggle back. Next door the wife returns but not the husband. And then one of the two sons. They wait.

I wait, too.

And then I hear him. He steps gingerly up the attic

stairs and peers around the corner with his wide green eyes. Romulus.

I can tell the moment he is certain of me. Suddenly his purr fills the room. I've never heard a cat squeal with joy, and yet that is the sound he makes as he leaps into my arms. He cannot get enough of my hands, my skin, my hair. He is breathing me in, tasting me with his whiskers, his tongue, his nose. Finally, he relaxes into me with a weight I never felt when I held Wynonna or Ashley. Though a tenth the size, he feels heavier even than Jerry Lee. He has the weight of a cat come home.

Romulus, dear, dear Romulus. How did you ever survive?

———

Back before all of this, Brattleboro, like an opal, was fire and light, ceaseless animation within a milky stone. The downtown brick buildings stood shoulder to shoulder on either side of Main Street. Protectively, the Connecticut River draped a sinuous arm around the entire community.

Once filled with pedestrians, Brattleboro resembled an embryonic, dewy-cheeked New York. There was Manfred the cross-dresser, always smiling, there were those in flannel shirts ten months of the year, and those perennially in Birkenstocks. There were cyclists in spandex and bikers in leather. There were the tattooed. And the ponytailed. There were kids hanging out near the parking garage. And kids hanging lights at the youth theater. There were lawyers in clunky winter boots and real estate agents first in line at the American Association of University Women book sale. There were poets sitting on milk cartons outside the food co-op. There were plumbers singing opera in the basement as they clanged on pipes, and cardiologists acting on local stages. There were homeless sheltered at church, and battered women sheltered in plain sight in neatly manicured neighborhoods. There were the walking dead, those human husks from the sixties, burned out on acid, who talked to themselves and haunted the streets at all hours of the day and night. There were those who would give you the shirt off their backs. And sometimes did. Right there on Main Street.

You couldn't take more than a few steps without passing an artist, a writer, a musician. Sometimes tempers flared but mostly it was a peaceable kingdom.

Where are they all now?

Will Manfred ever wave from a float in the Fourth of July parade again?

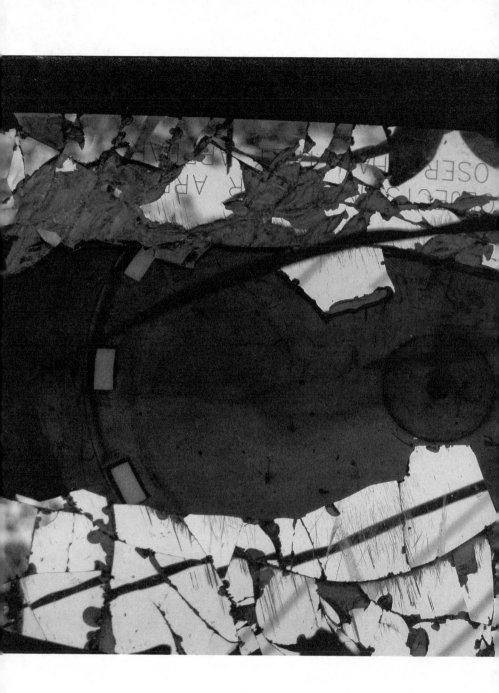

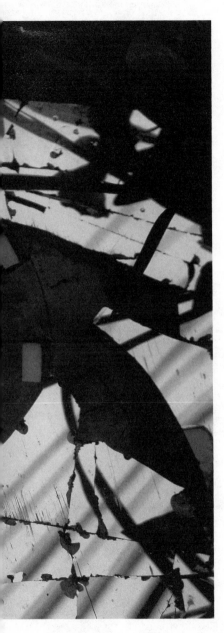

I sit on the bare floor in the attic with a shard of mirror in my hand and the photo album, studying the faces of my relatives, comparing their features with my own in the ragged glass.

I feel them all crowding inside me.

If I angle the glass in the morning light I can see an aunt nod to me in the mirror. I can see my grandmother beckoning. A cousin sticks out her tongue at me and grins. My mother frowns at me disapprovingly.

"What?" I ask her. "What do you want from me?"

"Get out of the attic," she says. "Go. Live."

"Not until you come home," I tell her. "You come home first. Then I'll live."

I'm being watched. I know the trouble is supposed to be over but I can't shake the feeling that I'm being watched.

My mind wanders with crazy ideas, trying to understand why I am still alone. Have they stopped caring? Has the time away from me convinced my parents that I'm not worth returning to? And then it suddenly occurs to me that perhaps my parents are in no hurry to get back because they think I'm still safe in Haiti. Or maybe right now they are in Haiti themselves, trying to find me, to bring me home.

Yesterday, next door, the second son returned. The cries of joy reached me through the closed attic window, sang through the glass, filled me with a contagious elation. I am so happy for them.

Now they wait for their last, their only unaccounted-for member.

When will *my* parents arrive? When will it be *my* turn to celebrate?

I still can't shake the feeling that I'm being watched.

The offerings at the Dumpster improve. Perhaps it's a sign that things in general are getting better.

But things are not improving for me. I don't know how much longer I can survive this floating, attached to nothing, to no one.

At the Dumpster there is this guy. I know him, I'm sure I know him, but I can't think straight. My head feels so hollow, except for a drumbeat of pain marching through it.

In the night I hear someone enter the house. Quiet, unfamiliar footsteps, not the footsteps of my parents. Whoever is here is exploring, from the basement up. I remember Celia and the man who raped her. Have I been able to protect myself all this time, only to be assaulted now, in my own home? Clinging to Jethro's bear, I shut myself into the secret room behind the attic wall.

Later, when all is still, I come out from my hiding place and move like a ghost down the stairs, through every room.

I discover the guy I saw at the Dumpster. He has curled up in the blanket on the floor in my room. He sleeps there. Romulus sleeps with him. I know him. Why can't I remember how I *know* him? He makes me think of the boys in Haiti. I think maybe he is from Haiti.

He doesn't frighten me, in fact I think he is a friend. I don't challenge him. I don't throw him out. I don't even wake him. I am certain he won't hurt me. But my brain will not cooperate. It will not reveal who he is. My skin hurts.

Soundlessly I climb back to the attic and enter the secret

lair, pulling a blanket over my rattling bones. I'm suddenly so cold. So cold.

———

Sometime before dawn, lightning fills the attic with a white terror.

A thunderbolt claps so close to my head it deafens me. My heart sputters. I think I am going to die now. Alone.

My mother is not here. My father is not here. Romulus is not here. Celia is not here.

I wait for the lightning to touch its scorching finger to my throat.

The boy from Haiti opens the hatch to the secret room, exposing me fully to the storm.

"Who are you?" I scream over the crashing thunder.

"Julian." He sounds quiet, calm despite the storm's manic energy.

Julian. Julian! Not from Haiti. From the apartment across the street. Julian from Burundi.

"How did you find me in here?" Terror transforms my voice; it is as white as lightning.

"You have been screaming," he says. And then he puts his arms around me. "You are burning up with fever," he says.

I have been on fire for days, but suddenly, in Julian's arms, the feeling of free floating comes to an end.

Julian makes a bed for me out of a pile of blankets and pillows and clothes. Over the next few days, he prepares meals for me. Gives me medicine. He never leaves me alone unless he's going after something to make me better. It's like my first days with Celia.

I start to recover. I wonder how Celia, after being so sick, got up and started walking again.

I can barely prop myself up without feeling utterly exhausted. Julian sits on the floor beside me, our backs against the wall. To pass the time we study my mother's photographs in her published books, the ones I hid in the crawl space.

"Some of these images are so happy, others break my heart," Julian says.

"Yes," I agree. I'd never realized how many of my mother's images depict pain and decay.

Julian is quiet for a moment, then gently he asks, "Was your mother sad, Radley? When I saw her she always smiled. Was that a mask?"

I remember my mother's laugh. Even when I heard it over the phone it made my heart leap with joy.

"No," I say. "My mother isn't sad. But she understands sadness. We won't look at these anymore if you'd rather not."

"Please," Julian says. "They help me."

I push the book away. "They don't help me. I don't want her pictures. I want her. Where is my mother?"

I rest my head against his shoulder.

"Why haven't they come back yet, Julian?"

And he tells me.

"It was bad here from the moment the APPs took office. So many protestors. So many young punks. I do not know where they all came from. I do not think they were all from here.

"The National Guard and the police, together, could not handle it all. They were under orders to uphold the peace. But they could not be everywhere at once."

Julian holds me as he talks. "A gang came after me, Radley. Not just me, everyone in our building. They knew about us, that so many of us came from other countries. They hunted us down. I was so frightened. I did not think such a thing could happen in America. Your mother, she heard us screaming. She came out of your house with her camera. I do not need to tell you how she was with that camera. Your father had been working around the side of your house. It took him a little longer to come out to the street. When he saw that we were being attacked, he tried to calm things down. But your mother would not stop taking pictures. The thugs yelled at her to quit. They threatened her. They swore at her. But she would not stop.

"One of them had a gun. He shot her.

"He did not know who she was, Radley. As she fell, your father came on like an enraged bull.

"The same boy, terrified now, fired again.

"He shot your father, too."

258

"My parents?"

"For a moment, everything stopped," Julian said. "They were only kids, Radley. Kids with guns. They stared at the bodies of your parents in the street. They forgot about us. And they ran away.

"By the time the police came there was nothing anyone could do."

"When did this happen?"

"Late in April, I think. It has been hard to keep track of dates."

By the time I left Haiti my parents were already dead. That darkened spot in the middle of Channing Street was the blood of my mother, the blood of my father.

I go out after Julian tells me these things.

I go out into the purple dusk.

I go out alone.

I touch the place in the street where my parents fell. I lie down and put my cheek there. Just there.

If someone drove up Channing Street right now my life would end . . . where the life of my parents ended.

But no one turns onto the street.

I lie there for ten minutes, twenty minutes, I don't know how long, and no one turns onto the street.

Julian finds me there.

He lifts me and leads me back up the front walk and through the broken door.

Julian no longer lets me out of his sight. He moves me from the attic, back to my own room.

"I knew when you came back from Haiti, Radley. I saw the police look for you, to tell you about your parents."

"Not to take me?"

"Not to take you. Why would they take you?"

Why would they take me . . .

"I watched you leave that night. I knew you were going. I wanted to follow you. I started to follow you. But I did not think you would want me along. I thought if I came it would make things more difficult for you."

"So you've been here, living on this street all this time? How? How did you manage?"

"I come from a place where one must learn to survive. When your country started to break down, I hoped it would not last long. I hoped that law and order would be restored. And it has been. Mostly."

"But how did you do it, how did you stay sane with no one to talk to?" I ask.

Julian shrugs, and it makes me think of Celia, and suddenly I break down.

My parents are gone. After all these months hoping to find them, they're gone.

How can I still be here? How can anyone still be here when my parents are gone?

———

Y ou've been taking care of Romulus the entire time."
Julian nods. "After your parents died . . . I came to your house. I took your mother's wallet from the front hall so it would not be stolen . . ." Julian hands the wallet to me.

My mother's battered black wallet. I always planned to buy her a new one. But I always changed my mind at the last minute, knowing how attached she was to the ratty old thing. She was funny that way. It suited her because it held everything she needed and still fit into her pocket. I slip it into my own pocket, wrap my fingers around it, and vow to carry it with me from now on, wherever I go. There is so much of my mother in it, so much of my memories of her in it.

Holding this thing my mother held, I feel the grief rise up again like floodwater; I sink into Julian's arms.

"Romulus came to me the moment I entered the house," Julian says softly. "He came home with me that night and has remained with me ever since."

"Did you use my mother's money to help pay for his care?"

Julian looks at me, puzzled. "I have not opened her wallet, Radley. It was not mine."

———

I try to distract the persistence of my grief. I thought my world would end when Chloe died. But this is even worse. I ask Julian about Burundi. He does not wish to speak of it. That's okay. I cling to whatever he *does* want to talk about. He is my life preserver. Julian understands, I think, the danger I'm in. The danger of drowning.

He asks me about Canada to get me talking. And slowly I tell him my story.

He loves best when I talk about Celia, and Our Lady of the Barn, and my excursions through the countryside.

Julian says, "Ah, Radley, to have had such an experience."

"Ah, Julian," I say back, "to have never had it."

A fat envelope is pushed through the mail slot, through the door that Julian has repaired. It is not restored to the standards of my father, but the door is more or less in place. My father would understand.

The envelope sits for some time on the floor in the front hall.

Finally we open it.

Someone wants to buy the house. They are offering cash. The enclosed papers have been drawn up and signed by a local lawyer. They look in order.

Julian and I sit in the dark, the offer for the house between us.

"It's a lot of money," I say. "When I was in Haiti I dreamed of having this much money. It is more than enough to do everything I dreamed of."

"But if you give up the house you will have nowhere to go," Julian says.

"Oh, but I do have somewhere to go. And I'd like it if you'd come with me."

I tell him about the pact Celia and I made.

"What about the rest of your family?" Julian asks.

"What family? My parents are gone."

"Cousins, aunts, grandparents . . ."

Julian, perhaps, is thinking of his own family, left behind in Burundi.

"We didn't have much in common before all of this. None of them have tried to find me. Celia is my family now. You. And Celia."

We go out, hand in hand. We walk in the moonlight down to Veterans Bridge and look out over the Meadows. We walk along the railroad tracks, following the course of the river. We pick our way up Main Street, through the neighborhoods, up to the reservoir on Chestnut Hill.

"Can you give all this up?" Julian asks. "This has always been your home."

It takes me a long time to answer. In the space between Julian's question and my reply my life plays out inside my head. So many of the images are my mother's, her photographs: Christmas in the house, walking in town after a snowstorm, sunsets over the Meadows. But so many more are my own: hanging out with Chloe, putting makeup on in the hall mirror, reading in bed. Memories wakened by Celia this summer in the games we played, in the stories we told. When the images finally end I realize my life here has ended, too. My parents are never coming back.

I nod. "I can give it up," I say. "Can you?"

"It is not mine to give up. I am not even legal in this country anymore."

I begin to laugh. "Is anyone legal in this country?"

Julian tilts his head back to look at the sky. His eyes

glisten. His nearness brings me such comfort. I don't love Julian. Not in the way I think he cares for me. I don't think I ever can love Julian that way. But what I feel for him goes straight to my soul. It is much like the love I feel for Celia. A strange, deep, holy thing.

We stand for a very long while, side by side.

I will always feel haunted here, no matter how much time passes.

"Let's sell it," I say.

My father kept meticulous records. Regularly checks would arrive for my mother's work. Each payment was recorded in my father's elegant handwriting, each column filled and tallied.

The money went into several accounts, but after my parents were murdered, the APPs, through some obscure loophole, appropriated every penny of it.

Perhaps this new government will restore what was taken from me . . .

But I have no proof, no account numbers, no codes or keys. I saved my mother's photographs, but not my father's account books. It's all gone.

At least I have my passport. At least I can prove I was their daughter. This, I think, and the proceeds from the house must be my legacy.

The things from the attic crawl space we transfer to a small storage unit at the edge of town. I've arranged with the bank to pay the rent on it indefinitely. Julian closes and locks the door on these precious few remnants from my old life. I am unable to do it myself.

When we finally go, I carry Jethro's bear, my mother's wallet, and a few changes of clothes. Julian carries Romulus. And whatever else he thinks we might need. We take a bus north to Newport with just the packs on our backs.

My parents always prided themselves on traveling light. They would be so pleased.

part four

I cannot cross the border with you," Julian says. "My papers are not in order."

I smile as we walk through the gritty streets of Newport with Romulus poking his nose out of Julian's backpack. "I'll get you over."

I am a different person now, walking along Lake Road into winter instead of spring, and this time I have Julian at my side, not Celia.

Soon I will have them both.

The schoolhouse rests in the russet palm of November, tiny, defenseless in the big forest. Celia and Jerry Lee sit on the step, sharing an apple. Celia's head is tipped to one side, her eyes half closed. Her wild hair has grown long enough to tuck behind an ear, though it's too stubborn to remain there. She is wearing a heavy coat but the roundness of her belly draws my eyes instantly.

"I've been waiting," she says softly.

Jerry Lee gives one of his doggy chortles and bounds down the steps to greet us.

———

Later, Julian and Celia, Jerry Lee, Romulus and I sit in Our Lady's barn, quietly waiting.

A stooped woman enters. She goes about her chores. When she is finished, she hobbles over to us.

It is the first time she and I have met face-to-face. Her skin is deeply lined, like a worn road map. She extends her hand to me. "I am Madame Seville."

Shaking hands with her is not enough. I extend my arms and she allows me to draw her into a hug, to hold her close. Her bones feel old and fragile beneath her coat. She smells of roasted hazelnuts.

Finally, Madame Seville speaks. "Celia prefers to pass her time at the schoolhouse but it is too cold to remain there any longer. Come. Please. You must all stay with me."

Between Celia and Julian there is an immediate connection. We spend day and night together but it is often Julian and Celia side by side, with me two steps behind. They walk together, exploring the countryside the way Celia would never do with me. Their heads bend toward each other. They are always talking.

After a few days Julian begins to tell Celia about Burundi. She listens quietly beside him and I feel like the extra beat in a rhyme, the one that doesn't belong.

I expect to chafe with jealousy.

But if there is any, it's unable to take root.

How remarkably fast our friendships shift and form and reform.

I cannot get enough of Madame Seville.

Julian and Celia cannot get enough of each other.

I wonder if, so many months ago, Celia recognized something she needed when she first found my mother's photograph of Julian and asked, guardedly, if he was my boyfriend.

The love growing between them makes it difficult to

breathe sometimes. It's as if they own all the air in the room.

They move back into the schoolhouse together, fixing it inside and out, installing what is necessary for comfort.

I remain in the farmhouse with Madame Seville. And slowly we begin talking, of everything, of my parents, and Haiti, and my summer with Celia. She speaks of her deceased son and husband, and the journey of her life.

Julian and Celia work together to repair the leaks, restore the floor I ripped out for the chickens. They install a stove, donated by one of Madame Seville's neighbors. And a privy.

Through the winter, as Celia's belly grows, as Julian and Celia make a nest for themselves out in the woods, I sleep across the hall from Madame. She teaches me to roast meat and bake bread, to sew curtains and make clothes.

We never use English when we're alone together. My French improves daily.

With a poker face, Madame instructs me in the proper way to tend chickens.

"Most farmers," she informs me, "do not hold their birds in their laps."

At first I think she is cross. That I have ruined Wynonna and Ashley.

And then I see the smile remake the folds of her face.

When my mother invited me into her kitchen I had no interest. Now, each day, I absorb everything Madame Seville does and says. She talks about her life on this farm, first with her parents, then with her husband and child, and now alone. We are making soup and baking bread. The day has been storm-gray with spasms of snow and a cold wind blowing. But now, as the afternoon wanes, the sun appears low in the sky, reaching across the worn kitchen floorboards.

I worry that we are too great an imposition on Madame Seville's solitude and her generosity.

"Thank you," I say again for the hundredth time. "Thank you for all you did for us this summer. Thank you for all you are doing now."

Madame Seville nods. "But you must stop thanking me, Radley. I did not take good care of you. I did not know there was Celia. I thought there was only you. I never left enough. I should have talked with you. I should have asked."

"It *was* enough, Madame. You kept us both alive. But I am worried. Are we asking too much of you now? And will it be too great a burden, all the extra work when the baby comes?"

Madame Seville frowns. "Celia will hardly need my help when the baby comes. She has you and Julian."

"It's just, Madame, that I don't think Celia knows how to be a mother . . ."

"Isn't that what *you* taught her, Radley?"

I stop stirring the soup and turn to her.

Madame Seville smiles. "You saw her through a terrible time. You were patient with her when you wished to walk away. You made her feel safe and cared for. She will be a good mother, because of you."

Madame Seville removes the bread from the oven. The smell of it makes me remember the first loaf she ever left for us, how completely that bread chased away our hunger and our despair.

And my mind turns to the orphans of Paradis des Enfants. I imagine baking bread for them, serving it warm from the oven.

Madame Seville's milky eyes drift over me like pale silk.

"I have so many regrets, Madame." I turn back to the soup pot and let the steam shroud my face.

"Radley," Madame Seville says as she taps the bread out onto a wire rack. "As long as you live, it is never too late to make amends. Take my advice, child. Don't waste your precious life with regrets and sorrow. Find a way to make right what was wrong, and then move on."

"But how do you make amends to the dead?"

"You are thinking of your parents."

I nod. And Chloe.

"Radley, you are so young. You have so much yet to learn, about yourself, about the world. The way you live your life now, that is how you make amends to those you have lost, that is how you honor them."

I stand over the soup and let her words move through me.

"Now, my young friend, go to the schoolhouse and fetch those two lovebirds and that clever cat and that saintly dog and tell them that dinner is ready."

And I do as she says.

Celia goes into labor one bitter morning in early February. Madame Seville and I have prepared a birthing room at the farmhouse, but Celia decides instead to have her baby in the little school, in the freshly painted back room that once had been Wynonna and Ashley's chicken yard.

Madame Seville and I know something is up when we find Jerry Lee at the farmhouse door, whining. I let him in and he runs up the stairs and hides under Madame Seville's bed.

"What is it?" I ask.

Madame Seville looks directly at me. "I think the baby is coming."

I throw on my coat and boots. Madame Seville hands me a doctor's bag filled with fresh towels and clamps, a sterile needle and surgical thread. I carry this assortment of birthing tools and together we follow the path to the schoolhouse.

Celia is unrecognizable. Her skin goes from deathly pale to an alarming purple depending on the state of her uterus. Her eyes glare through the agony of a contraction, then go dull and lifeless when the pain subsides. She's been laboring hard for about five hours Julian tells us when we arrive. Stubborn as ever, she suffers without complaint, unwilling to admit any weakness. But her desperation fills every inch of the little room, and I feel helpless to comfort her.

Do all women go through this to give birth? Did my mother go through this?

After an hour of relentless contractions, we see the head of the baby crowning, and then all in a rush she's here, in this world, screaming, turning a beautiful shade of pink. And Celia, who has been grimly silent through the entire ordeal, is suddenly laughing and crying as Julian holds this new life so tenderly that I know it doesn't matter about the biological father. Julian instantly accepts this baby as his own.

When it is my turn to hold her, Celia says, "Her name is Abigail." Holding the baby in my arms forces me to remain steady but I look searchingly into Celia's face and wonder why she chose *that* name. But when I ask, Celia, exhausted, just shrugs.

After a few hours, Madame Seville goes back home but I remain a little longer.

Jerry Lee returns on his own in the late afternoon. Abigail is nursing and Jerry Lee puts his head on Celia's knee to watch. Earnestly, he inhales the scent of this beautiful new creature in Celia's arms. It takes him less than a minute to fall completely under Abigail's spell.

That night, leaving Julian and Celia and Abigail back at

the schoolhouse, I curl up in my bed across the hall from Madame Seville and wonder what I would have done if I had had a child through all that has happened this past year. How would I have managed with a fragile, completely helpless infant like Abigail to keep safe?

Over the next few days, holding the baby, walking the floor with her, my thoughts return more and more to Haiti. Who is holding those children? Who is keeping them safe?

It is only now, because of Abby, that I finally realize what I need to do.

"Madame," I say. She is knitting a sweater for Abby. Watching her with the yarn, with the needles, I feel such a stab of sorrow, remembering my mom doing the same.

Madame Seville looks up, never missing a stitch.

"Madame," I say. "I'm thinking of going back to Haiti."

Madame Seville smiles. "Of course," she says. "Of course you must go."

She urges me to write to Monsieur Bellamy, to ask about the possibility of my returning.

———

Julian and Jerry Lee bring Abigail over the path from the schoolhouse for a visit each day. They arrive at our door with Abby's little face rosy from the chill air. But when I touch her tiny hands and feet they're as soft and warm as a fleecy pocket.

At the end of each day Madame Seville nods off in her chair, Romulus purring contentedly in her lap.

I remember my mother telling stories of how I would fall asleep over my dinner and she would lift me from my high chair, carry me upstairs to my crib.

I listen gratefully to the quiet, steady breath through Madame Seville's lips as she rests. She is yet one more person for whom my heart has expanded.

Celia, Julian, that beautiful miracle of a baby, and Madame Seville.

———

Celia and I pin up freshly washed sheets while Madame pegs diapers onto the clothesline. Sun shines through the fresh cotton weave.

Romulus and Jerry Lee nap together in a pool of April warmth beside Abigail's basket.

"Am I doing the right thing, going back to Haiti?" I ask. "Who else knows to carry Abigail like a little football when she has colic?"

"Well, we know *now*," Celia says.

"Abigail will have three of us to see to her every need, Radley," says Madame. "At the orphanage there are so many children and so few arms to hold them."

I remember thinking that same thing long ago, exactly that.

Back then the needs of the orphans overwhelmed me.

Their needs haven't changed during my absence, not judging by the enthusiastic response of Monsieur Bellamy to my letter.

It is I who have changed.

Canada has been very good about my status. And Celia's. And Julian's, too. They've forgiven our illegal entry. It is as if Canada is making an extra effort to model civil and humane behavior in contrast to the dismal example set by their neighbor to the south.

Abigail, born here, is Canadian.

Though I've yet to see a penny, the U.S. government has promised to restore to me all of the funds taken from my parents' accounts.

I'll have enough to help Celia and Julian and Madame Seville.

And still enough left to buy a small plot of land for the orphans. Enough to build a new home for them.

Madame Seville pegs up the last diaper just as Celia and I finish with the sheets. Madame comes around the clothes pole and takes my hand in her own. With one finger she strokes the skin on the back of my hand. I feel old sometimes, but when I look at our hands together, I know I am not old.

"Look at the good you have done here," Madame Seville says, smiling down at Abigail in her basket. "Imagine what you will do in Haiti."

———

Celia and Julian and Madame Seville present me with a farewell gift, a camera they've bought to surprise me.

"Take pictures of Haiti," Celia says. "Send postcards to us."

She smiles and wraps me in her arms while Julian

beams, holding the sleeping Abigail. Clever Romulus leans against Madame Seville's leg. It will be hard to leave him here, but I know he will be well.

I'm overwhelmed by their gift, so carefully considered, attained at such sacrifice to them all. The camera is small and used, nothing like my mother's equipment.

But for me it is completely perfect.

As I sit in the airport, waiting for my flight, I take from my backpack my mother's old wallet. At last I am ready to open it, to examine its contents.

There are her identification and membership and charge cards, some embarrassing old school photos of me, about a dollar in change and three twenties folded into tiny packets and hidden away behind a small, flexible mirror. I look at my mom's smiling face on her license. She must have gotten the photo taken in the summer. Her nose is sunburned. I stare into her eyes, smile back at her, realize how much I look like her. Her hair was really short when the photo was taken. The style reminds me of the pixie cut Celia gave me when we first got to Canada.

Just when I think I've explored every compartment, I find the edge of an envelope just peeking out of a narrow slit. It takes me a minute or two to wiggle it out of its hiding place. My name appears on the front of the envelope in my mother's handwriting.

All these months, without knowing it, I've been carrying around the last letter from my mother.

I hold the envelope in trembling hands. It's as soft as her skin. The paper has started breaking down from the friction of being folded into that tiny space. What was it doing there? Why was she carrying it in her wallet? Why did she hide it instead of mailing it?

I don't want to break the seal. Once the envelope is open it will be finally the end of my mother. But I'm too hungry for her last words. Too hungry to wait.

Carefully, I slide my finger under the flap and tease it open.

It's dated January 3. She must have written it as I was leaving for Haiti.

There is an oil smudge on the right hand side of the paper. I flash fondly on my mother's messy office and her butter bean salad. I rub the stain with my fingertips, then hold my fingers under my nose. But there is no lingering scent.

My eyes fall ravenously on the familiar slant of my mother's script.

My dearest child, it says.

> *If I live to see you fully grown, it can hardly make me prouder of you than I am today. You always had a grace of movement, even as an infant. Today that grace inhabits every aspect of your being.*
>
> *You never quite belonged to me, Radley. Not to me, nor anything or anyone.*
>
> *People gave you things from the time you were a little girl, surprising themselves and me, but never you.*

Whatever you wanted you received.

You could have turned cruel with that kind of power. Instead you've turned that power toward the healing of others.

I'll never comprehend the divine logic that put your life, your spirit into my arms. I think many times I did not deserve the privilege of being your mother. But that is what fate intended for us. And I am so grateful.

No matter what has happened or what is yet to happen in this crazy world, my darling child, you will find a way to go on and do such good.

Good luck, my beautiful girl, as you journey forward. Know that wherever you go, you carry my love with you.

Always and forever,
Mom

Whenever I traveled, Mom always slipped a note into my bag, something I'd find and read a hundred times while we were apart.

This, I think, was the note Mom meant to send with me to Haiti. I'll never know why she held on to it.

It's a mystery, like Celia choosing to call the baby Abigail. No one knew my mom's first name. No one.

The first night I'm back in Haiti, Jethro sleeps with his well-traveled bear.

Around midnight, one of the children appears at the side of my bed. I lift the blanket and she climbs in. She's cozy and warm from head to toe. She curls up against me. Her small body presses firmly into my own, as if she is attaching herself to me, like the dressing of a wound.

I wrap my arms around her and pull her close.

She leaves in the morning as the others begin to stir, but I feel the weight of her against me all day.

I am not certain who is healing whom.

Madame Seville would say, "It doesn't matter."

She's right.

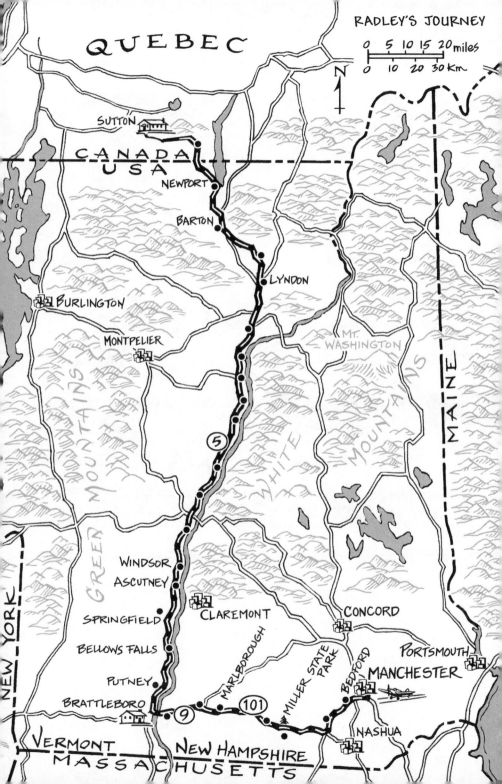

Acknowledgments

To Leda Schubert, faithful reader, intrepid friend, thank you for your invaluable insight and your unflagging support.

To Liza Ketchum, who has walked so many miles at my side. From the depths of my heart, I am so grateful for you.

To Mariam Diallo, who selflessly spends her discretionary time and money on the children at Orphelinat Foyer Evangelique. You are my inspiration and my hero.

To Sandy King, if I searched every corner of the world, never could a better cheerleader, shepherd, and courageous sidekick be found.

To Julie Reimer, you are one hardworking saint with an unsurpassed dedication to literature and the children for whom it is intended; a gifted reader, an extraordinary librarian, and a remarkable friend.

To Jean Feiwel, patience personified, vision beyond all imaginable distances, intelligence that sheds a light on every project, but particularly on this one, where so much was in the dark: my awe, my respect, and my thanks.

To Liz Szabla and Holly West, silent, but ever-present companions on this long journey, a quiet tip of the hat.

To Randy Hesse, how did I ever get so lucky?

To Paul Koch, political, historical, social, and ethical consultant, thank you for helping me see this world as only you could imagine it.

To Kate Hesse, lifter of veils on the actions and inactions of contemporary youth. How hollow this book would be if not for your input, and how grateful I am for your steady support.

To Rachel Hesse, reader of bones, fearless adventurer, befriender of those in need. Thank you for understanding and accepting my dazzling array of shortcomings.

And finally, to the children and staff of Orphelinat Foyer Evangelique in Haiti, you have taught me with your infectious zest for life that no matter how dire the circumstances, we always have a choice about how we meet the challenges and obstacles set before us.

For more information about the orphanage in Haiti that inspired Paradis des Enfants, go to: orphelinatfoyerEvangelique.org.

about the author

While Karen Hesse was growing up in Baltimore, Maryland, she dreamed of becoming many things, including an archaeologist, an ambassador, an actor, and an author. Over the course of her life, she has worked as a waitress, a nanny, a librarian, a personnel officer, an agricultural laborer, an advertising secretary, a typesetter, a proofreader, a mental health-care provider, a substitute teacher, and a book reviewer. And, throughout it all, she wrote.

She is the award-winning author of over twenty books for children and young adults, including *Letters from Rifka*, *Witness*, and *Brooklyn Bridge*. In 1998, she won the Newbery Medal for *Out of the Dust*, and was the recipient of a MacArthur Fellows Grant in 2002.

Now living in Vermont with her husband, Randy, Hesse pairs her love of hiking with photography, going out almost daily to record what she sees. When given the chance to enhance the reader's experience of *Safekeeping* with some of her photographs, she accepted without hesitation. Despite having a vast body of existing images to choose from, Hesse was determined to travel the entire route herself at the same time of year as Radley. As she describes it, "That long walk took place in the spring of 2011 . . . a very, very wet spring in New England. Undeterred, I dressed in raincoat, rain hat, and rain pants, Velcroed myself into an orange traffic vest, and exposed my poor camera to the most miserable conditions: rain, wind, fog, bugs, the buffeting of huge trucks. I believe this feet-on-the-ground research contributed to the authenticity of Radley's narrative. It certainly gave me insight I would never have had otherwise."

Visit Karen Hesse online at karenhesseblog.wordpress.com.